CW00485575

Patience and Courage

Patience and Courage

Book One: Stephanie Clover

RACHEL BRAMBLE

JANUS PUBLISHING COMPANY
London, England

First Published in Great Britain 2005
by Janus Publishing Company Ltd,
105-107 Gloucester Place,
London W1U 6BY

www.januspublishing.co.uk

Copyright © 2005 by Rachel Bramble
The author has asserted her moral rights

British Library Cataloguing-in-Publication Data
A catalogue record for this book
is available from the British Library

ISBN 1 85756 636 X

Cover Design Nathan Cording

Printed and bound in Great Britain

Dedication

To Sheila who has worked as
a social worker for 35 years and has
not received any recognition.

Chapter One

When your heart is broken the world seems like a daunting place.

Stephanie woke from a restless sleep. It was 3.40am and for the fifth night in a row she had awoken to a deep sense of loneliness. She had cried so much over the last few weeks. Family and friends were understanding but frankly were bored with her questioning. Steve had made his choice and there was nothing she could do about it and it was just like one of those stories in a women's magazine where the man runs off with the best friend.

Other friends said that it just wasn't meant to be, but that was easy for them to say. They weren't the ones who felt so alone. They weren't the ones who cried at the slightest smell that reminded them of Steve.

Some tried to make out that he wasn't good enough for her anyhow. They said that he wasn't her intellectual equal but it wasn't that which she missed. It was his touch, his cuddles, kisses and it was the way that he made her laugh. And he did, he was always clowning around. There had never been a dull moment when she was with Steve.

For eight years she had thought that her life was sorted. They had made so many plans together. They had bought the house and had both been promoted at work. They had a close group of friends and they should have been married last Saturday. She had cried so much on that day. It should have been that fabulous day that all the magazines and films tell you about, but instead it was awful and to add to it, it had been the most beautiful sunny day and they had forgotten to cancel the photographer.

He had turned up at the church to find no one there and had called Steph's mum in confusion. They paid him of course, begrudgingly, and her mum had said under her breath, "Make sure that this doesn't happen again", as if she did this kind of thing every week.

She decided to load the dishwasher. It seemed rather daft having one for her lonely plate and glass. It wasn't that she wasn't eating but just couldn't be bothered to cook for herself and so over the last week had become an expert on different cold meats and salads. They tasted OK but she did miss Steve's cooking; he was a good cook. He made a real mess, which she grumbled about clearing up, but now she looked at the clean work tops and missed the dried up marks. She had often left the clearing up until the morning as the nightly passions had taken hold of them.

She could understand if these had waned but they hadn't. They had always both enjoyed that closeness together. She tried to think why he had suddenly fallen for Kate. He had known Kate before he knew her. Kate had always been in their lives and she had shared with them her series of unsuccessful love affairs. But this time when she needed comforting instead of turning to Steph, which she had done so many times in the past, it was Steve that she had turned to. He had said that he couldn't help it, she was so vulnerable, Kate needed him. But she needed him too.

He told her that he didn't mean it to happen and when he found out that she was pregnant he had to think of the child too. He couldn't let the child come into the world without a dad, surely she would understand. She knew how he felt about not knowing who his dad was. He said that she would find someone else, she was a lovely person and there were loads of men out there just looking for someone like Steph. But on this cold February morning it just didn't feel like it. She wrote some emails to some friends. They had got used to the early times and always wrote back during the evening of the following night. She had even got the vac out and dusted the TV. She must have had the cleanest TV in her street. Some nights she had watched the late night films just to postpone going to bed, but she found that she still awoke at 3.40am and was a living wreck the next day at work and so instead she went to bed after the ten o'clock news knowing that she would have to renew her water bottle in the early hours.

She had always been hot and yet yesterday she had succumbed to buying a higher tog duvet instead of rubbing her chilled skin in the middle of the night and for the first time in nearly a decade she had had to buy some pyjamas.

So she stood shivering, waiting for the kettle to boil for her water bottle, and wondered whether her heart would ever stop hurting.

Chapter Two

Steph had had a busy day at work and was feeling tired. Sue had asked her to go out with her and her fellah to the pub but she didn't feel like playing gooseberry. She had done too much of that recently and so she decided to have a nice hot bath and settle down with a Chinese and a bottle of plonk.

She popped to the Chinese on the way home, only to find that it was shut. She had forgotten that it was Tuesday and so she scraped together what she could find in the fridge and succumbed to toast with lemon curd. It wasn't that she was fat but she felt guilty when she piled on the butter.

She abandoned the idea of the bath. She just couldn't be bothered. She felt like that a lot of the time these days. She just couldn't be bothered.

The phone rang and it was her friend Emma. She chatted to her and during the conversation Emma mentioned that Steve and Kate had had a little girl and they were going to call her Rebecca. Steph thought that the news would have upset her, but it didn't. She had been invited to their wedding but made excuses not to go. It wasn't that she didn't wish them well but how could she see the man that she loved and her best friend, whom she loved too, so happy when she felt so alone and miserable. She would just spoil it for them. She knew it was just one of those things. She and Steve were just not meant to be together. But it was just so hard to get used to.

She took a bite of her lemon curd toast and an advert on the TV caught her attention. It showed an old lady being visited by a social worker and described what services she had later received. She thought of her own nanna and how she had helped her mum care for her until her death just a few weeks before Steve had made his announcement. She didn't know what made her cry more, Nanna's death or Steve leaving.

She remembered how Nanna used to wander off and the police would call only to ask once again if the family needed some help. At times she felt that her mum should have asked for help. She had tried to help as much as she could but it was not like living with Nanna for twenty-four hours a day.

One year her mum and dad had put Nanna into a home while they had a week's holiday but when they returned Nanna acted up so much that they decided never to do it again.

She watched the old lady; she even looked like Nanna. At the end of the advert it said "Could you help Kate?" She thought of all the names they could choose it just had to be Kate but then she thought perhaps this was a sign, perhaps she was supposed to do something different with her life. She had found herself getting increasingly bored both at home and work. Her friends had told her that she had to get out more and in fact only the previous week Sue had said how boring she was getting. "He's only a bloke," she had said, "nobody has died." At the time Steph had thought that this was a bit insensitive bearing in mind that it was less than a year since Nanna had died but it was just a slip. Sue was well meaning. She had even gone on a blind date to please her, with a guy called Clive, but it was awful; she just sat there comparing him to Steve and although he was a nice bloke she just couldn't see a future with a thirty-nine-year-old accountant who had been collecting Toby jugs since he was eighteen years old. Sue had thought that she would do better with an older man but the eleven years difference just seemed too much.

Later that night as she filled her water bottle she thought about Nanna and the old lady on the TV. She wondered whether there was a heaven. She really didn't know what she felt about such things. She realized that she really didn't have a strong view one way or the other. It just didn't matter.

Chapter Two

She settled down for yet another sleepless night but this time it was different.

Chapter Three

Steph didn't tell anyone, not even her hamster, who she had bought at a time when she was feeling particularly broody. Steve had thought it was funny.

"How can a hamster replace a baby?" he had said, but he liked to play with Hammy the same as she did.

Time had gone on and Steve's baby was now six months old. She was a lovely little girl and the day that Kate asked if Steph could babysit didn't seem too awful. Yet again, she wondered about other people's sensitivity but then perhaps it was just that she was too sensitive herself.

She didn't tell anyone, so the day that she got the letter saying that she had a place on the course was one of the most exciting days of her life, because it meant that she could cope on her own. She just didn't need anyone any more. She began to enjoy life again and went to the pub with the girls.

Her boss was taken aback when she gave in her notice.

"What on earth do you want to be a social worker for?" she had said, as if she was joining the unclean. "You had a good future here."

But she knew that she had made the right decision and began to be grateful to Steve and Kate for turning her life upside down.

Steph babysat for them willingly now and carried baby Rebecca to chat with Hammy. She said that she would buy Rebecca one of her own some day when she was older.

Kate announced that she was pregnant again and Steph thought, how awful to have two children so close together. She had longed for the day when she and Steve would have a baby but now she just looked forward to her new life.

On the day that she had the interview, a few weeks after seeing the TV ad, she had driven to the university in her Fiesta and was lucky to find the last parking space. The receptionist had been very welcoming and had directed her to the ladies' toilet, It was a long time since Steph had had an interview and this one was different anyhow. She was to have both an individual interview and a group discussion. The course details had given some possible areas that the discussion would follow and Steph had looked carefully at the course outline for other clues. She had become aware of the large number of areas covering different forms of discrimination and so thought that there must be something on that, and sure enough there was. She had been asked how she felt about lesbian women adopting babies. She found herself in the depths of a very interesting discussion and came away feeling happy but not knowing whether she had said the right thing or not.

She opened the letter and read those words and thought, no, it's not a lemon curd sandwich for me today, its definitely time for one of those enormous custard tarts (that she loved and Steve hated). And she thought, this is my life and I can live it whatever way that I want. She set off for her mum's to tell her the news.

Chapter Four

That morning Steph got everything out of the wardrobe and tried a combination of clothes together. She decided on a pair of plain black trousers and a blue sweat shirt. She didn't know whether jeans were appropriate but also didn't want to wear a skirt. She would have to wait and see and go and buy some clothes. She had always been good with money and had negotiated with the building society to pay less money each month for her mortgage.

Her boss had agreed to give her a few hours' work a week, which she could do from home, and she was very grateful to her. "Well, when you find it's not for you we'll be pleased to have you back," she had said but Steph knew that she would never go back. No, she had a new life now and she was going to make the best of it.

She arrived at the assigned room ten minutes early and found three other people who all looked as nervous as she was feeling and suddenly a calm came over her.

"Are you sure that's what you want to do Stephanie?" her mum had said. Her dad was much more nonplussed. "Let her have a go," he said. "There's no harm in it. She can always go back to her old job if it doesn't work out. At least it's better than being lumbered with two young kids," he remarked.

"We managed," Mum had said and a discussion followed about how he thought that Mum would have been happier if she had followed her dream career first. Dad emphasized how he had no regrets and loved Steph and her sister Clare dearly, it's just... She knew exactly what he meant and as she sat listening to the course tutor outline the introductory programme, she had no regrets. This is what she wanted to do. She wanted to be a social worker and nobody was going to stop her.

She knew that it would be hard studying again and that most of her friends thought that she was mad joining such a fuddy duddy group, but she was going to prove them wrong. She was going to make them realize that what she was doing was worthwhile and she just wanted to be needed.

She thought of Nanna again and her mind flitted from her to the young woman shopping with a very young child carrying a big bump, she was only a child herself.

Yes, she could do this and suddenly it was her turn.

"I'm Stephanie Clover," she said, "and I have decided to train to be a social worker to do something worthwhile with my life." The words sounded naff as she spoke them, but then that was exactly how she felt. She didn't say that she wanted an adventure and that she wanted to meet lots of new people along the way because she didn't know that that was actually what she wanted. For now she just wanted to do something worthwhile.

She looked around at her fellow students and she noticed the ones that squirmed when she said these words and the others who appreciated what she said. The tutor was obviously very experienced as she just supported Steph's comment.

At the tea break she chatted to a couple of women who seemed roughly the same age as herself. One had had lots of experience working with children in children's homes. The other, like Steph herself, was fairly' new to it. She said that she had a baby at sixteen years old and had recently separated from child's father. Her daughter had started senior school the previous September and now she felt that she could do something for herself. She had been studying for A levels and was now ready for a university course.

Steph thought how different these two women's lives were to hers. She was glad that the only thing that she had to worry about was making sure that she had enough money to pay the mortgage.

She went back to room B22 and sat in the strange seats with a hook on desk that made you feel like you were sitting in a baby's high chair and then she saw him.

Chapter Five

There was just something about him. Well actually he was stunning. "He's gorgeous," the woman sitting next to her whispered.

He was about five feet ten inches tall, very slim, had short, straight dark hair and a goaty beard which made him look Shakespearean. His blue eyes flashed with excitement when he talked. He talked with a slightly posh accent with a bit of a stutter like Hugh Grant. Its soft tones sent shivers down Steph's spine. I'm in love, she thought, and then thought, Stephanie Clover pull yourself together.

He introduced himself as Alan Taylor and said that he would be teaching social work law. "I tend to get good results," he grinned and as he did this Steph became aware that all of the female members swooned. She even suspected that the two women who had announced in the introductory session that they were lesbians and looked adoringly at each other looked at him in that way too. They were a couple and had decided that they would train to be social workers before they had a child together.

Steph sympathized with lesbians and gays but didn't understand them and wondered how they would manage to produce a child. She was rather innocent when it came to these things.

Alan Taylor asked her to share experiences she had of the law. She said that she really didn't have any. "Clover," he said, "what a fine name you have. Stephanie Clover and a social care lover," he joked. Everyone squirmed as he said this, including Stephanie. "He might be gorgeous," she thought, "but if that was his level of humour then he would certainly never be for her."

The day came to an end and Steph found herself at home – tired, with many things to think about. She had a stream of calls asking her how it had gone, including one from Steve. She heard his familiar voice but felt nothing; she just thought of that man with the awful humour.

No, I'm not going to fall for him, she thought. Besides, there were several women in the group who were far more attractive than her. He was probably married, gay or in a long-term relationship anyhow, she thought.

She had popped into the university bookshop at the end of the day and had bought three books on the reading list. She sat down to read about the origins of social work and, as she read, she realized how little she knew of the career she had now chosen. In two years' time she would be a qualified social worker but today, her first day, she just felt like an ignoramous with a crush on the law tutor.

Chapter Six

The phone rang and woke Steph with a jolt.

She heard muffled sounds down the phone and couldn't make out the voice. "Is there anyone there?" she said. All she heard was her voice being called. "Steph, Steph." She realized that it was Kate. "What is it Kate? You sound awful." For the next few seconds she couldn't make out the words. All she heard was sobbing. "I'm coming round," said Steph and she threw on some clothes and her shoes.

The ten minutes' drive around to Steve and Kate's house seemed endless. She wondered what had happened.

She knocked on the door but found that it was already open. Kate was sobbing in the hallway but Steve was nowhere to be seen. Steph bent down to Kate and put her arms around her.

"Where's Steve?" said Steph. "In there," Kate pointed to the bedroom.

Steph left Kate in the hallway and walked towards the bedroom. Steve was sitting in the rocking chair cuddling Rebecca and rocking. He didn't notice Steph as she walked in. Steph saw that Rebecca was a strange colour.

"Give her to me" she coaxed… "No," said Steve and carried on rocking her.

A few minutes later Steph heard Kate's mother's voice

"Where's Steve?" she said but there was no reply.

Steph put her arms around Steve and he cried.

"It's not what you think... You know I wouldn't hurt her... We were just going to bed and I found her... she was cold and blue... She's dead Steph," he sobbed... "she's dead. I just couldn't get her to wake up."

"What's going on?" said Kate's mum walking into the bedroom. "Oh no," she screamed, "my baby Becky."

The next morning Steph arrived in the law lesson bleary eyed.

"Had a good night on the town?" said Alan Taylor sarcastically. Steph ignored him; she just felt a dull ache.

At the end of the lecture her friend Sindy asked her if she was OK. "Actually I'm not," she said and told Sindy about her experience the night before. "How awful," Sindy said. "What's awful?" said Alan Taylor peering over her shoulder.

"Well if you really want to know," said Steph in an angry voice, "my friend rang last night in a distressed state and I went around to her house to find her husband, who was my ex-fiancé, cuddling their dead baby. Does that make you happy?"

"Steph, don't," said Sindy.

"Its OK" said Alan Taylor in a subdued tone.

The next few weeks were stimulating but hard work. Steph didn't realize how tiring studying was. She went home and started again, reading the course books or writing essays. She still went to the pub with her girlfriends, who showed varying degrees of interest in her course but none of them decided to have a career change like she did.

Rebecca's funeral was awful. The coffin was so tiny and Steve had lost a lot of weight. Kate was heavily pregnant but neither she nor Steve showed any interest in the forthcoming baby.

Steve started taking sick leave and was finding any work at all difficult. In fact, family members were concerned that he was having a breakdown. Steve's mum said that it would have been different if he had stayed with Steph. She seemed to blame Kate for Rebecca's death. And yet amongst all this misery Steph felt personally contented. She had made the right choice; she loved being a student and she could also even tolerate Alan Taylor. Since she shouted at him he had been more subdued and, in fact, she felt a little guilty about it.

One day she arrived early at his law class and he was sitting alone quietly in the tutor room. After a few minutes she thought it was strange that he hadn't at least acknowledged her existence. "Are you OK?" she said.

"Sorry," he replied. "My thoughts were miles away. I'm leaving." "Where are you going?" she said, suddenly feeling a little unsettled about his remark. "I've got a job with a law firm in the States. Its quite a while since I practiced. I have been studying US law and have been lucky to get this job, starting in a couple of months' time."

"So why are you so sombre about it?" she said. "You should be pleased to get such an opportunity."

"I am... it's just..." She watched him hesitate. "Its just leaving the UK, I suppose, and going to the States alone."

"So you don't have a partner to take with you?" she said.
"No," he replied rather mysteriously.

Steph decided not to ask any further questions. Other students had trickled in during the conversation.

Chapter Seven

It was at Alan Taylor's leaving do that Steph met Luke. He was a PhD student who was undertaking some research into the effects of several moves on children who were being fostered and/or living in children's homes. Steph didn't really understand what it was about. All she knew was that she fancied him and when he asked to see her the following Thursday she felt excited at the idea.

Luke had blond hair and was very tall. He towered above Steph and had the build of a rugby player. When she first saw him he was wearing a black and blue rugby shirt. He looked Scandinavian and she could imagine him coming from a family of Vikings. He spoke with a Geordie accent and had moved to Birmingham from Newcastle to attend university.

The last time she had been on a date, besides the disappointing evening with Clive, was about nine years ago when she had started going out with Steve. She was twenty-eight years old and really didn't know what the dating etiquette was any more. When did you have your first kiss? And did you jump into bed on the first date or wait? She just didn't know. She rang her friend Sally, who never seemed to find the right man and had been very jealous of her and Steve. "I wish I could find my Steve," she had said, "it's not fair." Every man that Sally went out with was a potential Steve and then a few days later there would be another one.

"Sally, what do I do?" she said. "What are the rules?"

"I don't know why do you ask me?" Sally mentioned. "I'm not actually an expert."

"But you've been out with a lot of men."

"So is that what you want to do, to go out with a lot of men?" Sally remarked.

"I don't know" said Steph in a childlike voice. "All I know is that I have a date with a dishy guy who is four years younger than me."

"Oh, you cradle snatcher," Sally giggled. "Just be you, that's all you can do."

Fortunately, Steph was busy at the university. She had several assignments to complete and the course was preparing students for going on placement. She didn't really know what placement she wanted to do, there seemed to be so many areas of the work that she could go into.

Firstly, did she want something with social services or with a voluntary organization? Did she want to work with adults or children? She was on the last intake of the DIPSW. She had to keep remembering what it meant. The Diploma in Social Work.

There were so many things that she had to remember, so many things to think about. Sometimes she was scared to say the wrong thing. What if they thought that she didn't like some section of the community. She had been brought up in a white working-class family and had not really known any black people. Of course she had seen them around and there had been a couple at work but she hadn't really been friends with them. She began to wonder whether she was prejudiced or not. There were just so many things to think about.

Steve had been around a lot recently; he said that he just wanted to talk to Steph, she understood him. But when he turned up an hour before she was going out to meet Luke she found that her patience was running out. "Go home to your wife," she said, and she shut the door on him feeling a little guilty.

"You can't take the whole world on your shoulders," Jane, Steph's new friend from the course had said. "You won't survive as a social worker if you try to sort out the whole world." She had been a social work assistant for years and had at last got the secondment that she had been seeking to undertake the training.

"I think you should work with older people this year and try for the Social Services Children and Family team next year," Jane had said "and then you can keep your options open for a future job."

But now she felt guilty pushing Steve out of the door and so she rang Kate just to say that he had been around; she wished that she hadn't.

"He told me last night that he still loves you Steph and that he wished that we hadn't married."

Steph just didn't know what to say and found that her reply was just inadequate. She knew, however, that she certainly didn't want Steve back. She had entered a new world and she liked it. It was stimulating, exciting, a bit frightening but she liked it.

Chapter Eight

Luke was sitting in a window seat in the Royal Oak; he waved as Steph approached him. "Have you been waiting long?" she said. "Not long," he said, but later admitted that he had arrived half an hour early.

He chatted to her about his research, she found it interesting but was even more interested in his large brown eyes.

"I must be boring you," he said, "talking shop all of the time. Tell me about you."

"What do you want to know," Steph replied, suddenly thinking how dull her life had been.

She told him about her work as a secretary and how one night she had been watching the TV and saw the ad that had brought her to the course.

"I expect that the government would be pleased to hear your story," he said. "It shows that their advertising has worked. Most people I know come into social work because of some happening in their life. I started doing the DIPSW but gave it up. I knew that it just wasn't for me; I haven't got the patience to deal with people who can't get their act together and sort themselves out. I know that I've had a privileged background but I can't make excuses all my life for it. I can tell people what its like, tell the kids stories."

"Have you never thought of being a journalist?" Steph quizzed. "You could work for a large national newspaper and tell your stories."

"I have thought about it," he said. "My cousin works for *The Daily*

Conscience but for now I like the university life and I get to meet cool women like you, Steph."
Suddenly Steph felt a little uncomfortable and wanted to run away. How had she been taken in by his looks, she thought.

"Anyhow tell me about you," he said, as if he was a reporter, not from *The Daily Conscience* but from the *News of the World*. "What brought you to social work, surely not just an advert on the TV. Now, let me guess."

She found herself switching off. She thought of Steve and his sadness and then she found herself thinking of Alan Taylor many miles away. She wondered whether he had found himself a nice American woman to share his life with and then she heard the familiar sound of her phone receiving a text. She fumbled in her bag and read the text. It was from Steve; they had had a baby girl and were going to call it Stephanie, named after their best friend.
"Good news I hope," said Luke. "Yes, my friends have just had a baby girl."

"Oh, I like kids," Luke said, sitting closer to Steph. "But its even more fun practising for them," he remarked. This was Steph's cue. "I must go," she said. "I've got a lot of work to do, I'll see you around," she said as she walked briskly out of the pub, not giving Luke a chance to say anything.

She arrived home to find three messages on the house phone; two were about the baby and one was from Sally. "Ring me," she said. "I want to know how you got on with the gorgeous Luke."

"It was awful," Steph said, and described the situation. "And when he said the bit about liking babies and practising – well, I just squirmed."

"I bet one day he'll work for the *News of the World*," Sally joked.
"It wouldn't surprise me," said Steph.

"I know this gorgeous guy," Sally started saying.
"No, not now. I just couldn't hack it," Steph said. "I think I'll stick to nights out with the girls," she said. "Besides, I'm really too busy at the moment for men."

"You could try the internet," Sally said. "I've known a few people who have been very successful. I've never had the nerve myself and wouldn't be very good at selling myself but it might work for you."

"Perhaps, when I'm forty- five with two kids and a divorce I will," said Steph, "but for now I'm just happy as I am in my new world."

"Yes it sure sounds exciting," Sally said, "I wish I had the nerve to change but if I don't find a chap soon I'll be stuck on the shelf."

"Oh Sally, you are so old fashioned," Steph said. "You are only twenty-five years old, you've got years to go, you'll find that magical guy, I'm sure."

"Well, I wish you'd find him for me, Steph, because it just gets so trying."

Chapter Nine

Steph sat nervously waiting for the instruction to start. She knew that if she didn't pass this exam that she might not be allowed to go on placement. She had found social policy difficult to understand and had failed the assignment. She was allowed to take it again but it was dependent on how she did in her law exam. As the seconds ticked by Steph thought of Alan Taylor. She had found his manner a bit unusual but he had been a good lecturer and she had learnt a lot from him. She wished that he was here now to help her. She so desperately wanted to get through. She had been offered a placement with the carers project, which looked really interesting. She would be able to do both case work and group work and her supervisor was an inspiring woman who had a thirty-year-old daughter with Down's Syndrome. She was only forty-eight years old and had told her that she had become pregnant by accident and married the father but when he found out that the child had Down's Syndrome he had run off, leaving her to care for her daughter on her own.

Steph really admired this woman for her inner strength; she had come through a number of other tragedies, including the death of her twin brother in a motor bike accident.

Steph wondered why it was that some people sailed through life with hardly anything happening to them and then other people seemed to have everything. There was a woman on the course who was blind; her blindness had been caused by a rare cancer for which, to survive, she had had to have her eyes removed.

The words she was waiting for were announced and Steph took a deep breath and opened the exam paper. She read the first question and sighed with relief, she knew the answer. She managed to plod her way through all of the questions and, as time was called, she felt a sudden weariness.

"Let's go for a nice cream cake," Fran said. Steph found herself munching through the now familiar custard tart and just hoping that she had done OK.

She had one more lecture for the day, she hadn't taken much notice of the programme and, much to her embarrassment, found herself facing Luke.

The tutor introduced him to the group and said that he was going to talk about his research. He looked across at her, giving a knowing look, but she looked away, fixing herself on Tom.

"Why did you keep looking at me?" said Tom. Have I got a spot on my nose, or is my fly undone or something."

"Oh, sorry, Tom. I just wanted to avoid looking at the speaker, that's all. You see I went out with him on a date."

"Oh, I see," he said with an all-knowing look.

"No, Tom, its not what you think; he turned out to be rather a pillock actually."

"Any questions?" Luke said looking directly at Steph. The tutor started the questioning, after thanking Luke for the interesting talk. Steph was just pouring out her tea when the phone rang. She answered it. It was Luke. "Can I come round?" he said.

"I'm not sure that that's a good idea," Steph said.

"I just wanted to explain," he said.

"OK," she said.

She was wearing her scruffy jeans and considered changing them. She would have done in the days when she was with Steve but she decided to stay as she was; besides, she wasn't going to give him a second chance. She couldn't fall for someone who was so arrogant, could she?

She thought of Alan Taylor and wondered why she had written him off so easily. She could have given him a second chance. He had looked so sad when she had seen him alone in the tutorial room.

Chapter Ten

"Steph, I was a silly fool, an absolute pratt," Luke said. "You must have thought that I wanted to jump you straight away... But it just came out wrongly. You see, I haven't been out with anyone since I split up with Ann, two years ago."

He told her about how in love he had been with Ann and how he had wanted to marry her and have kids but she was just playing him along and was looking for a rich man who would look after her. Steph began to feel sorry for him, but then began to wonder whether he was just good at telling a soppy story.

"So will you give me a second chance?" he said at the end of his story.

"I don't know," she said, "I'll have to think about it."

She had been hurt too much by Steve to go jumping into another relationship; maybe she would just play the field a bit. It had been so long since she had been free and she liked the feeling. She liked being able to do what she wanted when she wanted.

"Can I ring you sometimes?" Luke asked.

"Yes, that's OK," she said, not knowing that she might come to regret that affirmation.

The next night there was a message on the answer phone from Luke. She took no notice of it and got ready to go to the pub to meet her friends.

"So how's your love life?" said Lucy. "Are you seeing anyone at the moment?"

Steph said that she was having a break from men. She was enjoying the course and that men were certainly on a back burner for a while.

"Fancy going on to a club?" Jean said.

"Why not?" said Lucy. "You coming, Steph?"

Steph hesitated and then agreed. She couldn't remember the last time that she had been to a club.

She arrived home rather drunk

The next morning she woke up and found that she had gone to sleep in her clothes. Her head was thumping. She had a vague memory of the night before. Her clothes reeked of smoke and she found traces of sick on the duvet cover.

"Oh no," she groaned, "what on earth did I do."

The phone rang.

"Hi," said Steph in a croaky voice. It was Lucy at the other end. "You are alright then," she said.

"Why shouldn't I be?" said Steph.

"Don't you remember the guy from Liverpool and his mates?"

"Oh no, what did I do?" said Steph.

Lucy laughed, "Nothing... I'm just pulling your leg. You just drank too much that's all."

But it wasn't, because Steph suddenly remembered snogging with some slim bloke and him making all kinds of suggestions. She remembered giggling as if she was a young teenager again, but then she couldn't remember anything else.

"Well, I'm glad you're OK," said Lucy. "Got to go to get to work... love you," she said. She always said this at the end of her calls and Steph would always reply, "Love you too."

She had known Lucy since she was eleven, when they were in Mr Partridge's class together. Lucy had been a good mate but after she started going with Steve she only had occasional contact with her.

When she split up with Steve Lucy was one of the first people to come and support her, showing herself to be a true mate. Lucy was not particularly good looking and was carrying around too much weight but had a good heart. Steph was surprised that she hadn't been snapped up years ago by a good man. She would make a great wife and mother. Lucy seemed happy though and when friends quizzed her she'd say, "I expect he'll appear one day."

Steph noticed the red flashing light that told her that she had a message waiting. It was from Luke. "It's only me," he said. "Surely you are not still cross with me; ring me," he said.

Chapter Eleven

Steph stood nervously by the notice board and read the words that she so wanted to see. Stephanie Clover pass.

She was on cloud nine when she arrived at Steve and Kate's house. She had persuaded them to have a night out together while she looked after baby Stephanie. Steve looked very thin and pale when he opened the door. "Off you go," she said, pushing them out the door. "The two Stephanies will be fine together."

She looked at baby Stephanie as she lay sleeping in her cot and thought how peaceful she seemed. She remembered that awful night and the coldness of Becky, the child who had caused the split between her and Steve. She thought how different her life would be now if Becky hadn't come along and how grateful she was to her. Her mobile rang, it was Luke.

"You've been avoiding me," he said. "Is there someone else?"

"No, I've just been having time for myself. There isn't anyone." He sounded relieved.

"I just wanted..." Steph interrupted him.
"OK, I'll meet you for a drink. But if you go on about how good you are at practising for babies again I shall walk out and that's it. I'll never see you again," she laughed.

The weeks went by and Steph began to see Luke on a regular basis. He never propositioned her and in fact she wondered whether they would ever share physical pleasures together.

One of Steph's wishes had come true. She had introduced Lucy to Tom and they had got on like a house on fire. He had persuaded her to apply for the course and she had been accepted.

And now Steph was walking into the office of the carers project and was one step closer to being a social worker.

"Hi Steph," said Jane, her supervisor. "You have started during an exciting week."

"Oh," said Steph, showing interest.

"Yes, as well as having three new families to visit we have a support group which is going to be attended by the local MP. He has shown a real interest in the project and is an extremely nice man."

"That should be interesting," said Steph, but in fact she suddenly found it a little daunting.

That night she arrived home exhausted with a blinding headache. She opened the door to Lucy.

"You look awful," she said.

"I feel it," Steph replied. "You've forgotten that we were going out on a foursome, then?"

"Oh, completely," said Steph.

"Have you taken anything"

"Yes, some Disprin Extra; they work fairly quickly for me."

"Well, go and have a lie down, and I'll keep the boys occupied when they arrive," Lucy said.

"Why are you so early anyhow?" Steph queried.

"You have forgotten haven't you? I told you that my hot water had gone wrong and asked you if I could come and have a bath at your place."

"Oh, I remember now," Steph replied. She had had so many things to remember recently. Her head was beginning to clear and as she put her head on her pillow she found herself drifting off. The doorbell rang. "I'll get it," she heard Lucy shout. She then heard whispers from the hallway.

She walked through feeling so much better. She was pleased with herself. Her first day had gone well. She had got on really well with the first family that she had visited. The parents were in their early seventies and had a thirty five-year-old son. He was out at the day centre when she arrived. They told her that no one knew why he was disabled. He was a small baby and they think that he had just not had enough oxygen at birth. He was a nice lad, they had said, and she thought that they were obviously fairly protective of him.

He arrived back home and was friendly towards her but very demanding of his mother. He reminded her of her friend's seven-year-old daughter who would regularly interrupt their chats with a request for a drink, packet of crisps or other such things.

The parents had talked about their social worker and how well they got on with her. They knew that she did what she could for them but it just wasn't enough. As they were getting older they were finding it increasingly difficult to manage their son. Sometimes he would go into the most awful rages and they were actually frightened of him. On one occasion they had had to call out the GP who had called out the police. They so wished that the rages could be controlled but how could you force a thirty-five year old to take his medication.

He went for respite once every six weeks at the Grove but they found that this just wasn't enough. This was why they had asked the MP to come to the support group. He just needed to hear what they had to say and to go back to the government to ask for more money. If they broke down and couldn't manage, who would look after their son?

"I'm ready" Steph declared.

"Are you going out with wet hair?" Lucy asked.

"Why, does it look awful?" Steph replied.

"No, it looks fine," Tom said.

Steph always trusted Tom's comments. She liked him a lot. He had become a good friend but she had never felt anything towards him. She had thought perhaps at times that Luke had been a little jealous of him but then, as Lucy had said, perhaps it was good to keep him on his toes.

They parked the car in Lucifer Street. Steph had often wondered how it had got its name but nobody seemed to know. They passed the little old newsagent which seem to manage to keep going. A placard had been left out and Steph read that the Aussies had won the test match. Her mind drifted miles away and she found herself thinking of Alan Taylor. She wondered what he was doing.

Chapter Twelve

"Have you seen the paper?" Luke said, as Steph answered the phone early that Saturday morning.

"Why?" said Steph. "Which one?"

"Any," said Luke.

Steph popped around the corner to get a paper and there, on the front page, was a picture of the young man she had visited just a few weeks before. She read the article. Apparently, in a fit of rage, he had stabbed both of his parents to death.

As she walked in the door the phone was ringing. "I'll be round straight away," Luke said. "Tom rang me. He told me that you had worked with this family. I'm coming now."

The doorbell rang. Steph opened the door, a man and a woman stood there, he with a notebook, she with a camera. "So what do you think of Social Services now?" he said. Luke pushed his way past them and shut the door. Steph stood confused. "I don't understand," she said with tears running down her cheeks.

The phone rang, it was Jane. "Are you alright?" she said.

"The press have been here," Steph replied.

"I'm so sorry," she said, someone here gave your address out to them by mistake."

"That's OK," Steph said. "But its so awful."

"I know", said Jane. "I just can't believe it; they were such nice people and he was such a nice young man. I know he had his tempers but I just never expected him to do anything like this."

The enquiry shadowed the placement. The university had considered moving Steph somewhere else but Steph felt that that wasn't fair to the carers project. It wasn't their fault, it was nobody's fault.

Steph had found the press a bit of a nuisance but Luke had moved in with her and she had found comfort. She liked waking up in his arms and she began to wonder whether he was, in fact, right for her. He was a kind, gentle man and she did feel that she loved him but there was just something missing. She didn't know what that something was but she just knew that she wouldn't spend the rest of her life with Luke.

Then there was John, the hack. He had been sent by one of the Nationals to do a feature and had come knocking on her door hunting for a story. He had been chased away a couple of times by Luke and by the staff at the carers project but there was just that something exciting about him. He had dark, straight, rather scruffy hair and green eyes that sparkled the same way that Alan's did.

When he went back to London he had given her his card and had told her to get in touch any time. There was just something about him. She didn't like his arrogant manner but she found herself attracted to him physically.

"What do you think?" said Luke, "Which of these three do you like the best?" he said.

Luke had decided to decorate the living room. He said that it was too dingy. Steph had agreed but with her IT project due in that Monday she really wasn't interested.

She had decided that her coat needed a wash and so had gone through the pockets. Steve had always told her off for washing things with tissues in the pockets and so she tried hard to remember to empty them. In the left-hand pocket she found a small card. She recognized the name, it was John, the hack.

"If you ever fancy a few days in London," he had said, "give me a ring."

She had laughed when he'd said it but now she thought that she could do with a break and she also remembered how she felt when she saw him.

Luke had popped out to get the paint and she decided to have a break from the assignment. She went in the garden and watered the pots, feeling guilty that half of the plants were dying. She was a hopeless gardener. She took the card out of her pocket, twisted it in her hand and wondered.

"Hi John, this is Steph, you know, the social work student."

"Of course I remember," he said. "How are you?"

They chatted for a few minutes and then John said, "So when are you coming to stay?"

Chapter Thirteen

Steph couldn't believe it: she had finished her first year and had successfully completed everything. She could look forward to the next year, her final year with a clean sheet, but not a clear conscience.

Luke had been so loving the morning she had caught the train to London. How could she, she thought. And now here she was again catching the train to London and in three hours' time she would be in John's arms. She never thought that someone like her could do such a thing. How could she be in love with two men, but she was, wasn't she? She knew that she loved Luke but John was just so exciting and such a fabulous lover.

She had sat through the ethics lecture that day and had felt like a hypocrite. She had justified her actions by saying that both men were single with no commitments. John knew about Luke but Luke didn't know about John.

Of course, the fact that John had other women as well made her jealous, but there was just something about him. She had led such a sheltered life and never thought that she could do such a thing.

She had told Tom and Lucy. They had different views Lucy thought it was OK but Tom thought it was awful.

"How would you feel if I did that to you?" he said to Lucy. She laughed.

"But I know you wouldn't," she said.

"Why?" he said in a quizzical tone.

"I just do," she replied.

She was right. Tom would never do that, he adored Lucy and she him. They were the ideal match and sometimes when she saw them together Steph would remember how she felt about Steve.

Steve was still not coping with life and his relationship with Kate was a little rocky but she felt that they would pull through.

"Just enjoy it while you can," Lucy said.

Those words sounded like a warning.

"Who is John?" said Luke in a distressed state.

"Why?" said Steph.

"Because he's sitting in our living room demanding to see you."

"Oh" she replied.

That "Oh" gave away several weeks of secret meetings.

"Hi, darling, I thought I'd just pop and see you as I have a story near here to cover."

Luke stood across the room and stared at Steph, she looked away and didn't say a word.

She walked into the dark house. She was used to Luke being there to greet her and the house seemed so cold and quiet without him.

It was two weeks since the awful meeting between Luke and John. She hated John for just turning up like that; he knew that Luke didn't know about him and she realized then how she had been duped by him. She had been carried away by his charms.

She had hurt Luke and she just didn't know what to do. He had ignored her calls but friends had said that he just talked about her all the time. He wasn't angry with her, he was just sad.

She felt like the woman from hell and she was glad that it had happened during the summer vacation. The staff at the residential home where she had got a summer job didn't know anything about her personal life and she had kept it that way. She had learnt an awful lot in her first year as a social work student, both about herself and about life in general.

The awful murder of the Smiths and the forthcoming enquiry had made her realize how you just couldn't assume anything in life. She had never thought that someone like her would cheat and have two men at the same time but it had been exciting and they had both fulfilled differing needs. It was her fault that she was now entering a dark cold house and it was only her that could do something about it.

John still wanted her but she knew that she would have to share him with other women. He would never settle down. But did she want to settle down?

She was enjoying life and her independence but then her friends reminded her that the old magical thirty was looming and her biological clock seemed to tick faster when she cuddled baby Stephanie.

"Wouldn't you like one of your own?" Kate had said.

"Sometime, yes," Steph admitted but felt that that sometime was a long time away; besides she had her course and currently her work and she found that she was fulfilled.

Chapter Fourteen

"Could you go up the cop shop and bring Paul home again" said Heather.

"Oh, not again… What has he done this time?" Steph said.

"He's back to the old shoplifting; McGregors, this time."

Steph liked Paul. He had been in care since he was two and at eleven held the local authority record for both numbers of social workers and placements. He had ended up at the Orchard because all other placements had been exhausted. He had got on well at the Days but then another child had been placed there and Paul had one day, in a temper, wrecked their house. The Days were good about it but even they found that Paul was just too much of a challenge.

He had got on well with Steph but was cross with her because she was going back to university in a couple of weeks' time.

"I'm still going to be working here," she told him.

"But for how long?" he said. "As soon as you finish your course you will be looking for a new job."

Steph knew that that was true and she knew that Paul had had so many changes of people in his life. But what could she do about that?

Lots of workers had tried to help Paul and his mum. He was only in care voluntarily; she could take him home any time and on a couple of occasions had asked for him to be brought back home. But, after a few weeks, she couldn't cope again and she would bring him back to the Social Services office. He would return to the looked-after system. Steph often commented to her fellow students, "Does that imply that other kids don't get looked after?"

One of the things that she found so hard about social work was some of the daft terminology that had been sent by the faceless lawmakers in the department of health. Kids hadn't been in care, they were looked after.

She had talked to John about it.

One day John had rung sounding terribly serious.

"Lets get married," he said.

"What?" she said, bursting out laughing.

"I'm not joking," he said

"But why?" she said.

"I want to be respectable."

She had thought it so funny and John had got cross at her giggling down the phone.

"Alright, I'll ask someone else then," he said. And he did just that and they accepted him.

Apparantly John had been offered a job with *The Reader* and felt that if he had a wife it would improve his position. Steph found out that she had been the second person he had asked and eventually the sixth woman had accepted.

He was to marry two days before term started and invited both Luke and her to attend.

It was Paul that got Steph and Luke back together. Luke had been visiting Paul as part of his research and Paul had found out that he used to be with Steph. Luke had been careful to arrange his visits when Steph was not on duty.

The night he rang she was in the bath. She picked up the message; it said, "I've been a fool, I need to talk to you."

She rang him and said that it was her that had been a fool, not him.

Steph had chosen a lilac dress and Luke thought she looked beautiful. "You'll upstage the bride," he had said.

"Why are we going to this anyhow?" she said.

"Because then I'll be convinced that there is nothing between you," he said.

"You mean you want to torture me for my sins," she commented.

Luke laughed. They had talked for hours about their feelings. Chatting with Paul had made Luke realize that he really loved Steph and that he was a fool not to try again. He had even thought that if he had to, he would put up with her having another man in her life as well as him but he realized that she had made a mistake. She realized that it was just the excitement but that even that was beginning to wear off. Those weeks on his own had been so lonely, as they had been for her, and they really did get on so well.

Luke had applied for a post as a lecturer in the department but had not been successful. One day Steph was looking through *The Daily Conscience* and saw a lecturer's post in Australia; there was just something about it.

"What are you looking at?" said Luke.

"Oh just the jobs section, that's all."

"Have you seen anything good?" he said.

"Only a job for you… but I don't think that you would be keen on where it is located."

"Why? Where is it?"

"In Australia," she replied.

Luke burst out laughing. They never said any more about it.

John's wedding was good fun. It had to be, that was the way John was. He and his bride had invited all of their ex-partners along to the wedding. They decided to be open with each other, although she didn't know that she was John's sixth choice.

They had a traditional church wedding with all of the bridesmaids. Wendy came from a rich stockbroker family. In fact, all except Steph and John came from this kind of background and so Steph felt a little out of place with her Brummy accent and roots. Luke had lived in Surrey for a short time and so he fitted in.

As they sat waiting for the bride Steph watched the guests entering the church and then she had the most incredible surprise looking straight at her from the bride's side of the church was Alan Taylor.

Chapter Fifteen

"Hello, how are you?" he said holding her hand gently but for too long.

"I'm fine," she said, "but…" She was aware that she was blushing. She introduced Luke to Alan but still felt that her face was as red as a beetroot. "It's hot in here," she said.

"Yes," said Alan.

"Who was he?" said Luke. "You seemed embarrassed to see him. Is he one of your ex-flings?"

"You make it sound as though I have had dozens of men in my life," she said.

Luke just laughed; he liked to tease her but he also realized when he needed to stop.

Steph suddenly felt so guilty. She had often wondered about Alan Taylor and what would have happened if she had responded to his overtures. She had felt at the time that it wasn't appropriate. She was the student and he had been the tutor but they must have been nearly the same age. It was just that they had come from very different backgrounds. He was the clever Oxbridge man and she was the ordinary working-class Brummy.

She had never really talked to anyone at the university about her roots. Most people on her course had moved some distance from their home but she hadn't; she had only come a few miles from Northfield, where her mum and dad still lived. They had worried about her when she split up with Steve and had been very disappointed that they were not going to be grandparents.

Steph would be thirty next year and by that age her mum had produced two children. Her little brother David had been a menopause baby and was still only thirteen years old, only a couple of years older than Paul. He was a nice kid, with lots of friends, and wasn't into girlfriends yet.

Steph's two sisters, Clare and Sharon, were both married but neither of them had children yet and so Steph's mum was the longing granny.

Steph found out that Alan Taylor was Wendy's cousin. They had been brought up together like brother and sister and so he had flown back especially from the States to be at her wedding. It was Wendy's other aunty, Rose, who Steph had found herself sitting next to through the lavish reception, who filled her in willingly on this information. Steph had casually asked her if she knew who Alan was and the whole story came tumbling out.

Rose also said that there were many women who had their eye on Alan but that he didn't seem to be interested in anyone. He had been a very outgoing young man but seemed much quieter these days. He never mentioned anyone in his life but she wondered whether he had a secret woman in the States, perhaps an older married woman who he was having a secret affair with, she had said. Her husband overheard these comments and burst out laughing. "Oh, Rosie," he said "You have such a vivid imagination."

Steph looked across at Alan and he smiled.

They got home late. Luke didn't want to stay overnight in London, besides it was very expensive and they had paid out quite a bit of money on the outfits and the paint. He was getting on well with the decorating. Steph had offered to do some too but he said that it was a nice change from doing his thesis. It had to be completed by the next spring and so he spent more and more time analyzing the results of his interviews and had begun to write the introductory chapters.

Luke liked to work into the early hours and so Steph found herself creeping into bed on her own and waking up to a very tired Luke.

"This won't go on forever," he said.

"I know," she replied and she did understand but after seeing Alan again she began to wonder whether Luke was the right man for her.

One morning she woke up just as Luke was coming to bed. It was a Thursday and she had a full day of lectures preparing her to go on her second placement.

"Its finished," he said.

"What, the whole thing?" she said.

"Yes."

"But I thought you had until next spring," she said and its only September... you are ahead of yourself."

"No, I had to have an extension because I couldn't get the interviews done in time. Besides, I have something to tell you," he said cautiously. "I'm going to live in Australia."

Chapter Sixteen .

"What, he came out with it first thing in the morning? Just like that?" Lucy said.

"Yes" said Steph. "He wants me to go when I have finished my course"

"And what do you think?"

"I don't know. I don't want to hurt him."

"But you don't love him?"

"I do but... it's just..."

Lucy looked straight at Steph; it was as if Lucy knew about her secret yearning and regrets. Why hadn't Alan Taylor just stayed in the States? Why did she have to have her affair with John? And out of all of the women that he chose to marry the one who had accepted him had been Alan Taylor's cousin. Life was just too strange... just too full of coincidences.

She had seen him just for a couple of hours and it had just made her doubt all her feelings for Luke. Up until then she had nearly convinced herself that Luke was the man for her. He did make her happy and she felt at ease in his company but there was just that something missing.

She had no regrets about not taking up John's offer; she didn't want to share her man with other women. It seemed that he had chosen the right woman as Wendy was happy being a wife and ignored her husband's continuing flings. But now Luke was asking her to go to Australia with him as his wife and she just didn't know what to do.

"I know you can't come until you have finished your course but..."

That Thursday she had sat through lectures not really hearing any of the words. Her tutor took her aside to talk about her placement.

"I'm afraid that the team are not able to offer you a placement after all," she said. "They are two members down and just feel that they couldn't cope with a student and so we'll have to look for another one. I'm still pushing for an area office though as I think that that is the experience that you need. Would you be willing to travel to Walsall?"

Steph said that she would. She knew how precious any Social Services placements were. They said that there was a national shortage of social workers and yet students had such difficulties finding the right placements. She knew of several people who still had no idea of where they were going to go and the placements were supposed to start in three weeks' time.

"Steph we can't do anything with him... he's just wild...we've called the police."

Paul was shouting, swearing lashing out at whatever he could find. The police came and took him away.

"What will happen to him now?" Steph said.

"I suppose he'll be put in secure," Gill said. "There is nowhere else for him to go."

Paul had come home from school that day. He had been doing well and the teachers were preparing for him to be reintegrated back into mainstream. He was an intelligent child who, given a different upbringing, would be doing well at school but that wasn't the case. His mum had asked for him back again and it had been agreed that this time care proceedings would be taken out. Paul's social worker just knew that going home wouldn't work. But his mum had taken an overdose and was now being treated in a psychiatric ward. Her social worker had rung Paul's and had had a go at her. She had enough stresses without putting this one on her too but Paul's social worker had said that although she sympathized it was Paul who mattered most.

It was a sad case: Paul's mum was only twenty-seven years old, two years younger than Steph. Paul was one of six children, all of who had different fathers. Paul's mum was a drug addict who just was unable to kick the habit. Baby George had been removed from her at birth but no one had taken out care proceedings for Paul because he was safe in the care of the authority.

Steph thought that John should write about Paul and his mum, not about all the celebrities who really contributed little to society. She thought that the public should know that he had trashed the living room not because he was some evil child but because he loved his mum and, in her way, she loved him too but she just couldn't give him what he needed.

It had been a hard emotional day. Luke had offered her the world, her placement seemed never to materialize and now her mum was telling her that her brother had sworn at her.

The phone rang; it was John. "Hi babe, I'm coming to Brum tomorrow, d'you fancy a night out?"

She just couldn't believe it, there was John still trying to get off with her. He said that he and Wendy had an understanding.

Luke looked at her in a considering way. "What's up?" he said. She told him about the day and about John's proposition. "And what did you say to him?"

She told him that just the idea of it was repulsive to her. She said that John just seemed so insensitive. He was just looking for a good time and would give very little in return.

Luke seemed relieved but didn't say any more; he just gave her one of those lovely cuddles that she liked so much and she fell asleep in his arms.

Chapter Seventeen

The inquiry into the Smiths' death was held in private. It had made national news as the government had very little to offer in terms of stories and the idea of two caring parents in their seventies being so brutally murdered by their son was just too tempting.

Steph picked up *The Reader* to see what John had written. It was a much fairer, more reasoned article than she had expected and wondered whether she had misjudged him a little. Although he knew that she had been directly involved with the case he hadn't tried to get an exclusive out of her. "I just wouldn't do that to you, Babe," he had said. She was building a different kind of relationship with him. She actually thought that he was really in love with Wendy but that it just didn't go with his image.

Steph had got the placement in Walsall but she found the travelling from Selly Oak to Walsall rather tiring. Some of her friends had a placement just around the corner from home but she returned home tired and then had to start reading for her assignments. She felt that it was just too much going on placement and studying at the same time but she had opted for the last of the two-year courses and she would just have to plod on.

She had to go to the Social Services office to share the information she had about the Smith family. She had found it a very emotional experience. She had met them and their son three times and had admired their commitment to each other and him. There had been no question that they would look after him for as long as they could.

Only three hours before it had happened she had spoken to Mr Smith on the phone. He had asked her if she could pop by to help him fill in a benefits form. The Department of Social Security had asked for an update and he was a little confused by the form. She had agreed to visit on the Thursday but that appointment never took place. The memory of this phone call that seemed so ordinary seemed to stick eerily in her mind.

They had wanted the facts. They were trying to find out if there was anything else that they could have done but there just wasn't anything. How could they know that he would get that knife and go at them in such a rage.

When the police had arrived at the scene he had been sitting on the floor rocking Mrs Smith in his arms with blood stains all over him. The policeman who found him had reported him crying, saying "Mummy Mummy, wake up."

Steph felt tears flooding in her eyes when she thought of this. The press had blamed Social Services, they should have done more, they should have known but how could they.

John had been brilliant. "Of course you or anyone couldn't have done more," he said. "He was just a nutter." "So why did the press have to say those things, why did they have to blame someone?" she had asked John. "It was just a story, babe," John had said, "and nutters make good stories."

"But he wasn't," she tried to explain; she didn't know what he was but he wasn't a nutter.

Her mind wandered and she wondered what would happen to Paul. She knew the situation was different to Ben Smith because Paul had a good brain but he was so vulnerable too.

Luke had told her that she couldn't take all the world on her shoulders. He had told her to come to Australia with him. He had even suggested that she perhaps gave up her course, but no, she wasn't going to do that. She loved social work. She loved finding out about all of the people and their situations and in a small way she did make a difference. She knew that it was only a tiny difference but at least she could try. Her friends had been there for her through the bad times. Many of these people just had no one and it just wasn't fair.

Luke went off to Australia on 10th January. He had an early flight from Heathrow and so had stayed at the airport the night before. She woke up to a new day all alone.

Chapter Eighteen

The Turner/Coopers were all fat. Steph knew that she couldn't record her opinions. She had to record only the facts. But it was a fact. Suzie, aged ten years old, must have been at least 11 stone and only about 4 feet 8 inches tall so why did everyone seem to ignore the fact. Their house smelt horrible too. Every time she went into it she wanted to open the windows and have what her gran would have called an old-fashioned blow through.

Steph realized that since Luke had left she had become a bit of a slob and she had eaten too many custard pies. At 10 stone 4lbs she wasn't as heavy as Suzie and she was 5 feet 6 inches tall, but it was heavy for her. She had always been able to eat anything. Many of her friends used to say that she could get any man with her slim body and blond hair. They had said that she was good looking and one guy had said that with her rosy complexion she really was an English rose. She just needed blue instead of her green eyes.

"Come to the gym with me," Lucy said.
She had said this to her several times but Steph was always too busy with either university work or she was on shift at the Orchard. Working and doing a full-time course was tough but she had a mortgage to pay and had borrowed some money from her parents to pay Steve for his share of the house. She wondered if she would ever get her finances straight so when they offered her extra weekend shifts she readily took them up on it.

It was Valentine's Day and she had looked for the post before she went to uni but there was nothing there. She checked her email and there was a jokey email from Luke. He sent her all his love and said that he missed her. She missed him too but she had got used to coming home to an empty house. She thought of when she lived with Steve. He would appear with a tray full of her favourite treats and with a red rose. He had spoilt her and in lots of ways she had taken it for granted. She wondered if he treated Kate in the same way. She hadn't seen either of them since New Year's Eve when she had attended the family party with Luke.

Her mum had been charmed by him. "Oh Steph, why don't you go to Australia with him?" she had said.

"But Mum, I can't give up my course."

Her mum just didn't understand why it was so important to her. She could never be just a cleaner like her mum. She thought what a snob she was becoming. There was nothing wrong with being a cleaner. Everywhere needed cleaners. As a child sometimes she had gone to meet her mum at St Austells to walk the half mile back home with her.

She thought of her dad and how he had worked at Cadbury's since he was sixteen years old. He was an expert on Creme Eggs and could tell you how many different mixtures were made for different countries and their different tastes. She had never complained when he came home with a bag of goodies for them, but he and her mum had been very wrong about the "Snowflake".

"Oh, it's far too sweet," Mum had said. "Nobody will like it."

When her dad was called in to work extra shifts to increase productivity Steph had laughed.

"OK Lucy, I'll come to the gym tonight to keep you happy," Steph said.

Steph had popped to the university for her mid-placement meeting. She was doing fine and was heading for a pass in her course. She felt relieved because, with the placement starting late and initially not enough work to do, she had wondered whether she would get enough for her competencies.

Some of her uni friends were really struggling but Steph was lucky, she had Clive as her practice teacher and he was straight talking and no nonsense.

"I want to see what you can do with Suzie Turner," he had said.

She had been visiting the family weekly since November. Suzie wouldn't go to school. She had been bullied but the Head had sorted the bullies out.

Steph hadn't liked school much; she had been bullied at much the same age because, for a ten-year-old girl, she had had big boobs. She laughed about it now and often said that they stopped growing when she was eleven.

She felt sorry for Suzie; besides being fat she was really not that good looking or clever. She lived with her dad. Her two brothers, who were younger than her, lived with her mum three doors away with their stepdad and his three kids.

There had been suspicions that Suzie's relationship with her dad wasn't quite normal but Steph had realized that the particular social worker who made this claim tended to see sexual abuse everywhere. Most recently Suzie's dad had found a new woman in his life and she was planning to move in with him and Suzie, bringing not only her two children but also her daughter's baby.

Clive had asked Steph to do a family tree and an eco chart so that she could understand the family properly.

Steph began to realize how complicated some people's lives are. This placement had opened her eyes to a world she just didn't know. Everyone in her family had always worked; they might not have had particularly good jobs but they worked and they had always been very condemning of people who sat on their "lazy arses" and scrounged off the state.

"Why should I pay my taxes to pay for those fat lazy gits who breed like rabbits," her Uncle Henry had said over Sunday dinner only a few weeks ago.

Steph found herself trapped between two worlds. She realized that it just wasn't that simple. Suzie couldn't help being born into a family which had been labelled for so many years as dysfunctional. She wasn't particularly bright and so what could she do in life. Steph had become aware that so many social workers in the office just felt defeated. The system which imposed so much form-filling denied them the energy to think about what they could actually do to help change things for children like Suzie. She had missed so much school and the family that she belonged to had all been under-achievers so she too had been classed in this way.

It had been different for Steph. Her headteacher had told her parents that she must stay on and do A levels. She was just too bright, she had too much potential, they had been told.

Suzie's new sixteen-year-old sister had a three-month-old baby who was already on the child protection register. Steph planned to visit the family jointly with the other social worker when the family moved in with Suzie and her dad but today she sat with them on her own.

"So we'll go to the park shall we?" Steph coaxed.

"OK," said Brian, Suzie's dad, looking rather nonplussed. "Steph, when you come back will you help me with this form?" he said.

"OK. Come on, Suzie… let's go."

Steph sat on a swing next to Suzie; the walk to the park had been slow. Suzie obviously had never walked that kind of distance. Steph watched the couple of young mums with their children and wondered whether Suzie had ever been to the park with her mum.

"Did you used to come here with your mum?" she said.

"No," said Suzie.

"What did you used to do with your mum?"

"Nothing much," Suzie replied.

Steph watched Suzie observing the other families, she wondered what she was thinking.

"Tell me about school," Steph said.

Chapter Nineteen

"What's up Steph?" Lucy asked

"I'm pissed off, that's all."

Steph thumped the nearby punch ball.

"Is it Luke?"

"No, it's nothing to do with him. Its my placement."

Steph told Lucy how she had been called into the office by the team manager and had been given a real telling off.

"I only asked her about school; apparently there is a psychologist working with her who is deliberately not discussing school at the moment... but how was I supposed to know... nobody had even told me that she was working with her... there's nothing on the records about her existence."

"And what did Clive say?" said Lucy.

"He said that he forgot to tell me."

Steph had noticed that what she was taught at the university was far from the reality of social work. She had become aware of the huge differences in both the attitudes of different workers and how good they were at their jobs.

Clive was well liked in the team but team members and the secretarial staff would often make comments like "That's typical Clive". Everyone in the team had too large a caseload and Clive was no exception but his service users liked him and no one ever seemed to complain about him.

Clive was laid back. When Steph had told him what Martin had said he had told her not to worry, "Martin just panics, that's all, and is scared of Mary." Mary was the psychologist who had complained. Martin rang her and used his charm. But that wasn't the point; Steph was feeling angry. She wanted to do a good job and she felt that she had let Suzie down.

"Are we going for a bite?" Lucy said.

"No," said Steph, "I've got to get home."

She didn't have to get home, it was just that she wasn't feeling very sociable. She shouldn't have agreed to go to the gym. She should have just stayed at home feeling sorry for herself.

The phone rang. It was Mum. "Are you coming round on Sunday?" she said.

"Not sure, why?" said Steph.

"It's your gran's birthday, have you forgotten?"

Steph had forgotten. She got on OK with her dad's mum but sometimes she just didn't know what to say to her.

The phone rang again and Steph decided to ignore it and remain soaking in the nice bubbles that Luke had given her for Christmas. She wondered how he was getting on; she seemed to get fewer emails from him these days and wondered whether he was still that keen on her.

The door bell rang. Who was calling by at this hour, she thought. It was only 9.15 but even so nobody usually called unannounced this late.

Chapter Twenty

Steph had a hectic day on placement. Half of the placement days had now gone and she had proven to be a good worker and so the team manager had suggested to Clive that she could take on a larger caseload. Most students who worked in children and family teams had protected caseloads which meant that generally they worked with about eight families. Of course, it depended on how heavy the cases were. Steph now had twelve, including the Turner/Cooper family.

The social worker who was allocated to baby Cooper was on long-term sick and so as Steph was going into the family anyhow she was asked to report back on how he was doing. She didn't mind doing this as it meant that she could say to any prospective employers that she had worked on a child protection case.

Steph had learnt an awful lot about what it was like to work in a Social Services team. She had seen good workers in practice struggling with very limited resources and increasing bureaucracy. She had also seen disenchanted workers who seemed to be blasé and critical of the people they were working with. They were not as bad as Uncle Henry but they had received training and he hadn't. They seemed to see all people's negative traits and none of their positives. She had also learnt that although workers like Clive were nice people and well liked by their service users they were a perpetual nightmare to their managers as they could not be relied on to get their paperwork done in time.

Steph found that she was able to keep up most of the time. She had been to a funding panel and had successfully got funding for a disabled child and his family, this gave her a degree of self-satisfaction.

She had been to two child protection conferences and had seen how the different professionals worked together and how powerful some were compared to others. Yes, there were lots of things that she had learnt and, on balance, she felt that she could work permanently in such a team.

Although she had enjoyed working in the carers project the year before she felt that she could do more working with children and their families.

Her home life had become a little unsettled. She rarely heard from Luke. Steve and Kate were still rather up and down and she would often find one or the other of them ringing her for support or turning up at her door. And something very strange had happened; John had changed.

The night that the doorbell rang it was John. He had told her that he had split up with his wife. He had realized what a pretentious world that he lived in. He had been to work that day and found himself writing a story about the latest goings on of a celebrity and as he wrote he found that the woman that this celebrity was involved with illicitly was called Stephanie. He said that he had thought of Steph and what she was doing and it had suddenly dawned on him how shallow his world was.

He had thought that, working for *The Reader* he would be taken more seriously. He had played along with the shallow game, he had had the women, the pretty wife, the good life but there was something missing.

He had asked his editor about writing about more serious things but he had been told that there were enough reporters covering those stories and that he had been employed to lighten the paper with the more frivolous articles.

That evening he had gone home and found his wife in bed with their gardener. She just laughed at him and said, "For goodness sake, look at all the women that you have had, have I ever complained?

70

Besides, he's much better at it than you and has a bigger dick. If you don't like it you can get out and go to your beloved Steph."

He had packed a bag and she had laughed at him. "You'll be back," she said, and he had feared that he would. He had admitted to Steph that he was scared; he had lived this life for so many years and didn't know how to start again. He had just got in the car, and arrived at her door.

"Can you accompany Sarah this afternoon to the Lewis family?" Clive said.

"What time?" said Steph.

"Two o'clock."

"I have the Cooper case conference."

"I'll go to that and you go with Sarah, it'll be a good experience for you."

Steph felt unsettled; she was well prepared for the conference. In fact she felt rather disgruntled.

Sarah always seemed to need someone accompanying her. Mark had quietly expressed his view that Sarah rubbed service users up the wrong way. Steph had never been on any visits with her and so didn't really register what he was saying.

Social workers were supposed to work within a particular ethos but Steph had realized that there were so many different interpretations. When she had gone back to uni for her call-back days she had shared her experiences of her placement with her fellow students and had lost count of the times that she had heard others say, "Well, we don't do it like that." Sometimes these discussions had lead to blazing arguments and sometimes Steph had thought that the uni staff must be living in a different world.

"OK," said Steph, "I'll ring the family and the Chair to say that you will be there instead of me."

The family weren't happy; they had wanted Steph there because she understood them. She was honest and straight talking, but she said that Clive was good, he would do what he could for them. She knew that he was good but still felt miffed.

"Are you ready?" said Sarah.

"Yes," said Steph. "Are you driving or me?" said Sarah.

"Don't mind."

Steph ended up driving.

They were going to visit a notorious family. A family who had been known to Social Services for two generations. There were so many volumes on each child in the family that if you were given them you had the threat of long-term backache. It was Sarah's turn to have them, nearly everyone in the team had dabbled with them, except for Clive. For some reason he had never worked with them. Now she would see what notorious meant; she would be able to truly see and test out the values that she had been taught at uni and she didn't realize how her life would change.

Chapter Twenty-one

The house was what Steph expected, rather run down with a small gate that wouldn't shut properly and piles of junk out in the front. The front door needed painting and there was a board replacing a broken window.

Sarah knocked on the door and then stood back. She could hear shuffling behind the door and then a rather thin woman who looked in her forties opened the door.

"Hello, Mrs Lewis," said Sarah.

"You better come in," the thin woman said, and then shouted up the stairs, "Jim, the social worker's here".

They stood in the hallway and Steph recognized the now-familiar smell, which she found difficult to describe. It just seemed to be so prevalent in service users' households. Yet again she thought of her gran and how she, in the days when she was still "with it", would have swept through a house such as this opening all the windows and doors, and would have had some fresh-cut flowers to brighten them up. She would have told them that she would help them to get going and not let them slip into their shoddy, sloppy ways again. It was so different now. She knew that social workers had to bite their lips. They could tell the truth but it had to be a sanitised, politically correct truth. It just wouldn't do to say that someone's house stank. Mr Lewis came down the stairs and Steph was surprised to see a rather handsome, slim man appear. He looked a lot younger than his wife.

"So, whose this gorgeous woman you've brought with you today then, Sarah?" he said.

"Oh, sorry," Sarah said, "this is Stephanie, she is a student social worker."

Mr Lewis came rather too close to Sarah and Steph wondered whether he was actually going to touch her. It was obvious that he liked to be powerful and to dominate.

"Right, Mother," he said, "go and put the kettle on."

The rather thin woman scurried away obediently into the kitchen. "You are lucky to find me in, I've got a new job," he said, as they followed him into the living room.

Yet again, to Steph's surprise she found herself in an immaculately tidy room. On the mantelpiece and all around the walls were photographs.

"You seem to have a large family," Steph said.

"Coo er, she speaks," said Mr Lewis.

"Of course I do," said Steph.

"Well most social workers are scared of me and my brother; we both have kids under the Social, have done for years, I was in care when I was a kid."

"Why was that, then?" said Steph.

"'Cos my mum couldn't cope with me, I was a bit of a naughty boy."

"And you still are," said Mrs Lewis, bringing a tray with three cups of tea and a plateful of biscuits.

"Oh, darling, you've spoilt our cover. She's been playing the underdog for weeks now," he said, with a grin on his face.

Mrs Lewis went over to her husband sat on his lap; he squeezed her breast and then gave her a passionate kiss.

"Er, um," Sarah cleared her throat.

"Oh Mother, we better behave," said Mr Lewis, with a twinkle in his eye.

"Mr and Mrs Lewis, we need to talk about Jason and Tracey."

"Yes," said Mr Lewis looking intensely at Sarah.

"Oh Jim, behave," said Mrs Lewis giggling.

"Oh, it's just that Sarah looked so severe. So when are you taking them into care?" Mr Lewis said sarcastically.

"You know that we don't want that, but they just can't roam all hours and the neighbours are complaining of the noise, and…"

"Take a breath lass" he said.

Steph began to feel very uncomfortable; it was obvious that Mr Lewis was in control of the situation. Sarah was a shambles. He was just walking all over her. She felt so embarrassed.

As they left Mr Lewis winked at Steph. "You can call me Jim, if you like," he said, "What do you think Mother, Stephanie seems alright to me. Do you think we should give Sarah the sack and ask for Stephanie instead?"

"Oh, he's just impossible," Sarah mumbled under her breath as they arrived back at the office.

They hadn't talked much in the car on the way back.

Clive asked how it went and Sarah told everyone that Mr Lewis had said that Steph could call him Jim. The team then had a discussion about the family. Mr Lewis was one of three sons of Mrs Ryan who had been known to the department for twenty years. He, like his brothers, had been in care every time that Mrs Ryan got a new man in her life and then when she ditched them she would ask for the boys back.

Two of the boys, Jim and his brother Mark, had followed the family pattern of social work involvement. Their brother Steve had made a success of life. He worked successfully as a painter and decorator and had found a woman who seemed able to tolerate the ways of the rest of the family. Social workers had relied on Steve and his wife Marie to pull things together. Quite often they would take in Jim and Mark's children and work cooperatively with social workers only to have all the good work destroyed when the children went back home.

Jim was the charmer who got involved in all sorts of crooked deals. He had been in prison on several occasions for things such as driving without car tax and had dabbled with taking and pushing drugs but it was his brother Mark who everyone was really frightened of; he had a nasty evil streak which made Jim seem like a pussy cat in comparison.

Mrs Ryan still tried to control her boys and whenever there was a case conference she would come along. She had been with Bert Ryan for a few years. He was a placid man who said little. He went out to work having done the same job since he was sixteen years old and nobody knew why he had got together with Hilda. She ruled the roost but it was him who the boys respected.

Steph found all this information out from Dennis. He had worked with the family for some years before he went off on a secondment for a couple of years. When he came back to the team it just didn't seem appropriate for him to work with them again.

Mark had four children aged between six and fifteen. Jim had two children and one stepchild, a girl of twenty-two who had escaped the family and lived in Doncaster. Occasionally they would hear from her but most of the time she would keep away.

Steph arrived home wondering what she had been doing all day. None of her planned work had materialized. Clive had failed to get to the conference and an angry Chair had contacted Martin, the Team Manager. Clive was inaccessible and so initially the team manager took it out on Steph until Mark stepped in to say that Clive had insisted on the change of arrangements. Martin had gone back to his office grumbling. Dennis said that at the best of times he didn't get on well with the Chair but he'd get through it; he'd been through far worse things since he had been managing the team.

Steph asked Dennis what the worst thing had been. He said that a favourite member of the team had developed breast cancer and the team had seen her long suffering until her eventual death eighteen months ago. It had been hard on everyone seeing her trying to struggle on to support her teenage children.

Steph thought about all these pressures as she turned the key in the lock. She walked in the hall and smelt wonderful curry aromas coming from the kitchen. "That smells nice," she shouted to John and opened the kitchen door not to find John but Luke.

"Hi darling, I thought I'd surprise you." Luke rushed over to her and threw his arms around her.

Chapter Twenty-one

"When did you get back?" she asked.

"I got off the plane three hours ago and came straight to you."

"Oh, it's John that's cooking this, not me, he's a nice bloke after all. He told me that he is now lodging here. In fact, he told me a lot of things."

Steph suddenly felt guilty and wondered what John had told Luke. Over the last few weeks she had liked having John around; he had been good company and it was nice not coming home to an empty house. She had made it plain to John that Luke was her man and he hadn't tried anything on at all with her. In fact, he seemed so different to the man that she had first known. He was trying to write a novel and to get some cash to pay Steph rent and for food he was shelf-filling in Tesco.

Her friends couldn't believe that a top London journalist had given all of his life up to write what he wanted and fill shelves but he had.

"What did you tell him?" she said the next morning after Luke had left.

Luke had stayed the night and she had snuggled in bed with him but it just hadn't felt the same. She had been very aware of John being in the room along the corridor and so had found their love-making a bit restrained. It just wasn't as good as she remembered.

"I told him about my life in London and about my wedding. I told him that I had asked you to marry me. Why didn't you marry me, Steph? I just wouldn't be in this mess now if you'd married me?"

John seemed serious when he said this.

"You must be joking, John, you were bonking every woman you could get your hands on."

"I wasn't actually," he said. "That was a sham. In fact, after I met you I found it difficult to do it with anyone, including my wife."

"Oh come on John, don't say that you were in love with me."

"Of course not," he said in a rather unconvincing way.

Chapter Twenty-two

"He's back," Tom exclaimed.

"Who's back?" Steph replied.

"Alan Taylor."

Her heart missed a beat.

"I thought you'd be interested," Tom said, with a grin on his face.

It was the coffee break and they had agreed to meet up with Lucy. She was enjoying the course and had a bit of free time from her placement and so all three had agreed to meet at the university.

"Sorry I'm late," said Lucy, "I got a bit distracted."

"What have you bought?" Tom said.

"Nothing, actually. I went to the library and I forgot the time."

"Guess what, Luce. Alan Taylor, the gorgeous law tutor is back."

"Oh yes, I remember Steph telling me about him. Didn't he rub you up the wrong way or something, but really you fancied him like hell?"

"That was a long time ago," Steph said.

She thought of the day that he had annoyed her after baby Becky had died and the day when he told her that he was leaving to go to the States. She thought about the times when her thoughts drifted and she wondered how he was doing and whether he had found his dream woman.

"Time to go," said Tom. He leant over and kissed Lucy. They were a devoted pair and in many ways acted like an old married couple. Lucy seemed so happy these days and sometimes Steph wished that she had settled for a new life overseas with Luke.

Luke had decided that his new life just wasn't for him and had gone back just to organize his return to the UK. He wanted Steph to sell her house and buy one with him, but she said that that wasn't fair to John and that she would need time getting used to him being around again; besides, she wanted to complete the course, look for a job and then she would decide. She only had four more weeks of placement and everything was very hectic. She had told him that he would just have to wait.

John's declaration and Alan's return had unsettled her and she was wondering what she felt. She knew that she had to settle for one of them but which. Later that night she shared her feelings with Lucy over the phone.

"It'll sort itself out," said Lucy. "Perhaps neither of them are the right man and he is waiting somewhere in the wings."

Steph felt confused. She decided that the most important thing at the moment was her placement. As Lucy said, she really had to be patient and just see what happened.

Chapter Twenty-three

"He's back," said Mike.

"Who is?" said Steph as she walked into the Orchard.

"Your favourite lad, Paul. His mum is OK and she has agreed to him being freed for an open adoption with her having significant access."

"He's a bit old isn't he and who would want her hanging around?"

"Well, apparently there is some law tutor from the university who is in his mid-thirties, a single bloke who wants to adopt him. He knows the director personally and is trying to pull strings.

Steph just couldn't believe this. A law tutor in his thirties; surely that had to be Alan Taylor.

"Hi Steph, I'm back and I'm going to behave this time," said Paul.

"And how's Mum?" said Steph.

"Oh, we've had a good chat and both of us realize that we will never live together."

"That's very wise," said Steph.

Paul told Steph all about his time in the secure unit. He said that he had started writing to a lecturer who lived in the States, he had been introduced to him by Luke when he came to see him about his project and the man in the States had become a good friend.

"Oh, he's not after me in that way, he has been checked out by the university and my mum has met him."

"What did your mum think of him?"

"I reckon she fancied him but I think that he might already have a woman in his life. No, he's not gay or a paedo, he's just a decent bloke. In fact, guess what, he's coming here today. He should be here in a couple of hours and is gonna take me out this afternoon. I'm not sure what we are doing as he doesn't like McDonald's much."

Steph suddenly felt panicky; she wondered how she would cope with seeing Alan again.

"What's his name?" said Steph, trying to act casually.

"Alan," said Paul and Steph suddenly felt a strange giddiness. She quickly composed herself and went about the tasks of the day.

The next few hours until Alan came felt like a blur. She wasn't sure what she was recording about Paul and the other three boys that were living at the Orchard. She burnt some toast and said the wrong place when she answered the phone, giving the name of her place-ment rather than the Orchard, which lead to an initially confused but then amused colleague.

"Steph, this is my friend, Alan."

Steph looked up at Alan.

"I already know Steph," said Alan. "She used to be one of my students when I worked at the university. Are you ready then, Paul? Shall we go to McDonald's?"

"OK," said Paul, "but we don't have to."

Steph smiled at Paul and glanced at Alan as they got in Alan's car.

"Have a good time," she said.

"I met someone today that I haven't seen for a long time," Steph said to John as she stirred the sauce.

John was preparing some salad. They often ate together these days and would chat about what they had both been up to during the day.

"Who was that then?" said John.

"It was my old law tutor from the university. He went off to live and work in the States about six months ago. He was meeting with a kid I work with at the Orchard and it is rumoured that he wants to adopt him."

"Will he be able to do that and take him to the States?"

"No, because he's going for an open adoption so that the kid still has contact with his mum. That's interesting. I hadn't thought about that; so he must be coming to live back in the UK."

"Don't tell me, he's another of your conquests."

Steph stopped stirring and went and thumped John on the arm.

"What's that for?" John said playfully.

"You make out that I have loads of blokes."

John laughed.

She was thinking about Alan as she twisted spaghetti around her fork and the phone rang. John answered it. "How are you mate? Yes, oh yes, she's fine, here she is."

"Who is it?" Steph mouthed.

"It's your sweetheart, Luke," John said as he passed the phone to her.

"Hello darling, I shall be flying back to the UK on Thursday 22nd. Will you be able to meet me? I land at Birmingham at 7.20pm."

"Yes, that's OK, see you then, bye."

"So you have nine more days to play," John said.

"What do you mean?" said Steph.

"Well, it's pretty obvious that you don't feel that Luke is the man for you."

Steph looked at John in an enquiring way but didn't say a word. How could she deny it, because it was true. She hadn't been certain until she had seen Alan again. She didn't know whether Alan was available or not but whether he was or wasn't Luke just wasn't the right man for her and somehow she had to tell him.

"I'm right, aren't I?" John said as they cleared the table together.

"Have you heard from your wife?" Steph said trying to change the subject.

"Yes," said John, "she was talking about us getting back together but I don't want to be in that superficial world any more. She said that she doesn't either and that she is sorry but I just don't know what to believe."

"Sometimes you just have to go with your heart," Steph said and as she said this she knew that she would have to tell Luke the truth. She didn't love him and had never loved him and that there was another man who she had always been attracted to.

Chapter Twenty-four

Suzie Turner was still in bed when Steph arrived at the house. It was nearly twelve o'clock.

"Why is she still in bed?" she said to Mr Turner.

"She won't get up," he replied. "She says that there is no point, she is fat and nobody likes her."

"But she was doing so well at the new school, what happened?"

"She won't tell us. You go and talk to her Steph."

Steph went into Suzie's bedroom. It smelt stagnant like the rest of the house. Her curtains were drawn and half hanging. She had yanked them down a few weeks ago when she had a fight with her stepmum and obviously no one had bothered to hang them up again. There were piles of clothes lying in a muddle all around the room and no sign of any toys or things that so many ten-year-old girls had in their bedrooms.

Steph thought of some of the families that she had visited last year in her other placement. Children who were disabled but with adoring parents who cared so much for them. They would have felt so sorry for Suzie as she did. She thought about how the general public just didn't know what kids like Suzie were going through. Every year there would be programmes like Children in Need raising money for needy kids and the NSPCC would run their adverts showing sad-looking kids, played probably by rather wealthy young actors, but they really didn't know about kids like Suzie who lay in bed at twelve o'clock on a Tuesday when they should be thinking about what pudding they would choose at school.

She had talked to John about Suzie, she hadn't told him her name as she knew that she was bound by confidentiality. He felt sad for her but said what could he do? He felt powerless too. He realized that for twelve years since he had left university with a first class honours degree in English that he had been trapped by the bright lights of London and the world of journalism. He had wanted to get on and instead of returning from Oxford to his birth town of Manchester he had moved to London to a world that he had thought was so right for him. His Don at Oxford had suggested that he should go for *The Daily Conscience.* "Go back to Manchester," he had told him, "I have a contact who could give you some work; it's a start. But no, he had been drawn to London. Now at thirty-four years old he was reassessing his life.

"It's so awful" said Steph, "I just didn't know what to do, she's only ten years old and she knows that she is not the brightest of kids but just lying there in that room, it's just awful."

"What did Clive say?" said John.

"He said that I should just keep trying, but they are planning to have a case conference soon."

Steph found it hard swallowing her rice. John had made one of his lovely curries but she found it hard to eat and just picked at her food.

"Steph, you can't take all the burdens of the world on your shoulders," he said. "Lets get a soppy video out. What do you fancy?"

"You choose," she said.

They lay on different settees and picked at the bowl of cashew nuts that John had bought.

"I shouldn't be eating these," Steph said.

"Don't be daft," John exclaimed. "You are just lovely as you are and you can eat less tomorrow."

"Thank you," she said and got up and kissed him on the cheek. He put his arms around her and they sat together on the settee.

"Yes, Stephanie Clover, you are a lovely woman and whoever you choose as the love of your life will be such a lucky guy."

As he said this, the phone rang and Steph went over to pick it up.

"Hi, Mum," she said.

"It's Dad; he's in hospital, he's had a stroke."

They arrived at the hospital at ten o'clock. John had insisted on driving her.

"He'll be alright," he said, trying to reassure her. "Loads of people have strokes, it's usually a sign that they have to slow down or change their lifestyle. He'll be alright, you see."

Arriving at the hospital reminded her of the last time she had been there after baby Becky died. Such a lot had happened over the last eighteen months; her whole life had changed and here she was arriving with someone who was new to her life but increasingly important. John was such a good friend and she wondered whether he really was her best friend. She didn't see him as her man but she wondered what might have happened if the phone hadn't rung. But in lots of ways she didn't want anything to happen she just wanted what she had with John to stay as it was.

Steph's dad was lying in bed surrounded by family. "How is he?" she said to the nurse who was standing nearby.

"He's going to be OK; at fifty-seven he is young for a stroke and will have to watch his diet a bit but he has no slurred speech, just a bit of weakness in his hands and feet. We will have him up and with the physio in the morning."

"So soon?" said Steph, questioningly.

"Yes, it's best to get stroke patients up and going as soon as possible."

Steph went over to her mum and put her arms around her.

"The nurse has just told me that he will be fine," she said, trying to reassure her mum.

"I was so frightened, Steph, I realized how much I loved your dad and how awful it would have been if I'd lost him."

"Mum, you've got loads of time with Dad yet."

Steph's mum appeared to be reassured.

John stood away from the family, Steph looked across at him and felt that it just seemed so natural for him to be there and yet she wished that it was Alan who would be taking her home and reassuring her.

She looked across at her dad, who was sleeping peacefully, and realized that she too would miss him so much. For an instant she felt jealous of what her mum had, a man who loved her so much, but then she thought how silly she was. She was still young and her man would appear, she felt sure of that.

She walked along the corridor away from the ward and suddenly she saw Mr Turner and his partner. They looked very distressed.

"Mr Turner, are you OK?" she said, stopping to talk to him.

"It's Suzie, she's taken an overdose," he said.

"Oh no," Steph just didn't know what else to say.

As they arrived back home Steph just felt numb. She had been fighting back tears. She went to bed but couldn't sleep and went downstairs into the living room. John came in a few minutes later.

"I couldn't sleep either" he said and he sat beside her and put his arms around her. She began to sob. "Just let it all out," he said and she cried and cried.

"I need a tissue," she said and John popped to the toilet and brought back a toilet roll. "How inelegant," she said, half laughing and half crying.

Chapter Twenty-five

Steph found it quite interesting, the discussion about power and powerlessness. She had brought in an old article from *The Daily Conscience* that talked about the top one hundred people who had most influence on the government in terms of social policy.

"Do you realize," she said to Tom, "of the top one hundred, eighty-five are men. Doesn't that say a lot about why our systems are just so screwed up?"

"Oh Steph, I really don't want a great gender issue discussion. I feel guilty enough being a white middle-class bloke. What can I actually do about it?"

"You could back me up."

"Well surely, you could get your lodger to do that. Can't he get himself a job again? You said that he worked for *The Reader*."

"He did but he wrote celebrity stuff."

"Well, you'll have to try and convert him."

They walked back to the Lecture Theatre. All of the year group were meeting today at the final call-back day. As they passed room 222 Steph saw Alan Taylor chatting to one of the lecturers. He saw Steph and made his apologies to the tutor and came towards her and Tom.

"Hello Steph, I never got to say a proper hello when I saw you the other day. How are you?"

"I'm just fine," she said. "But I have to get to a lecture."

"Would you be free at the end of the day to talk about Paul?"

"OK. Where do you want to meet?"

"If you come to the social work reception I'll find us a room."

"What's going on then, Steph?" said Tom. "The law tutor goes off for six months to the States and returns only to talk with you about a mysterious Paul. I thought that your bloke is called Luke." He looked at Steph in a knowing way.

"He is. Paul is a kid I work with in my paid job who Alan is hoping to adopt."

"He's a single bloke isn't he?"

"As far as I know, yes, but what does that matter? Paul needs a good home and Alan could probably give him one."

"I still think that he would be better off with a couple," Tom said.

"But there isn't a couple who would be willing to adopt him as he can be a very difficult child. I am surprised at your traditional view after nearly two years of the course. Do you think that gay men and lesbians shouldn't adopt too?"

"Yes. Kids don't want to be seen as freaks, they just want to be like anyone else, they just want a mum and dad."

"But loads of kids don't have a mum and dad. You know what we have done in statistics; I can't remember the figures now but there is a huge number of lone parents. On the course half of the students are lone parents."

"But that's because social work attracts all sorts of misfits of society; no one sane would come into it, they can make loads more money somewhere else if they've got half a brain."

"Oh Tom, all that education and you still feel that way."

"Steph, I'm just being honest, that's all."

Steph didn't get to see Alan Taylor; he had been called out on an emergency, what exactly it was she didn't know. The receptionist just said that he was in a great hurry and had scribbled her a note.

Steph read the note. It said, "Sorry Steph, will have to catch up with you later. Say hello to Paul from me when you see him next. Ring me."

He had left his mobile number.

Steph slipped the paper into her pocket, she felt a combination of relief and disappointment. There was just something about Alan Taylor. There had always been something about Alan Taylor.

"Steph, you are such an idealist," John said.

"But don't you think that kids should be given a chance to be happy with someone who can really love them?"

"Yes, but Tom does have a point. People do stare at people who don't fit into the normal modes and if a kid had two dads what would he or she call them and what happens later when they bring their girlfriend or boyfriend home?"

"But surely all of those things can be sorted out."

"Some people could sort them, others would just compound the difficulties for the kids. Take your Paul, for example; he could get very close to Alan but then Alan could find a woman who didn't like Paul, or who felt threatened by Paul. Then what happens?"

"But that can happen in any family."

"I know it can, but the difference is that Paul isn't Alan's child and never will be."

Steph found herself getting angry; she just couldn't agree with what either John or Tom had said but then she thought about her own upbringing with a mum and dad who had been together for over thirty years and were still very happy with each other. Perhaps she was a hypocrite.

The phone rang. "It's for you John."

John took the phone, spoke and then looked very serious. He went out of the kitchen and shut himself in the living room. Steph wondered who it was, with John looking so serious. She had often overheard his conversations and knew most of his friends. He had a lot of friends from his years in London and some had come to stay.

"Well?" she said, looking at him quizzically.

"It was Wendy, she wants to come up for a few days and stay."

"But I thought you had decided that she was now history," Steph said.

"I suppose, I just don't know."

For the next couple of days John seemed very sullen. They sat at mealtimes and he just didn't want to say much at all. He never spoke about Wendy and Steph didn't bring the subject up. She was very busy with her last assignments and only had a couple more weeks of placement left.

She had a lot to take in.

Chapter Twenty-six

Suzie had spent a week in hospital and then it was decided that she would be better off with some foster parents on a shared-care basis. Her parents had agreed to this after talking it through with Steph.

"She just needs time to sort herself out," she said.

Steph knew that this was a half lie; yes, she did need time but also hopefully in time the family would realize that this arrangement was best for Suzie on a permanent basis. Most foster parents had kids on a full-time basis but Steph felt strongly that Suzie needed that time with her family. She was to live with the foster parents all week and then go home some weekends. She had only been there a short time but already she seemed a lot brighter.

The foster parents, Linda and Bruce Hollis, lived fifteen miles from Suzie's house in a village and Steph had managed to get Suzie a place in the local school. They had a daughter who was nearly the same age as Suzie. They had tried for other kids but had not been successful so they thought that fostering kids would give their daughter Charlotte some company. Charlotte was a nice girl and had made friends with Suzie straight away.

The day that Steph visited, Bruce had come home from work with a brand new bike for Suzie. Steph was a bit worried about this as she knew that Suzie's family would never be able to afford one but the link worker hadn't been worried.

"So what do you think of your bike then?" Steph said, looking straight at Suzie. She had learnt at uni about the importance of good eye contact.

"It's alright," said Suzie, eating a digestive biscuit.

"It looks great to me," said Steph, and then she thought that she should have not made a big deal about it.

"I don't know what me mum is gonna say, that's all," said Suzie.

"Do you have to tell her?"

"Course, I do. I tell her everything."

Steph suddenly had doubts. Had she done the right thing, moving Suzie from everything that was familiar to her? Later that day she talked in supervision with Clive about it.

"But, Steph what alternative was there? Remember how you felt the day you went round and found her still in bed, and what about her taking the overdose. She's only ten years old, she deserves a chance. Her parents just can't give her what she needs. When she took the overdose she was alone in the house, it was one of the neighbours who came round to get their ball back who found her."

"Oh, I never knew that. They didn't tell me."

"Steph, she could have been dead, they are lucky to see her at all."

"He's right," said John, while they sat watching *Holby City*.

They liked watching mindless tele together. John had been quiet for the last couple of days. She wanted to ask him about Wendy but she just knew not to pry, she knew that he just couldn't cope talking about her yet.

"Wendy's coming at six tomorrow," he said. "Will you be home?"

"Why, do you want me to be or not?"

"Yes, if you can. I don't think that I want to see her on my own."

"OK, I'll try to get back as quick as I can."

Steph sat next to John and they snuggled up together and watched all the programmes, including the news. At 1am Steph woke to find herself lying against John. He was fast asleep. She looked at him sleeping; he seemed so peaceful. She thought about him and how, as with Luke and Alan, her first impressions had led to very prejudiced views of them. She didn't know Alan very well but she realized that she fancied him like hell. She had thought that John was an arrogant, loud-mouthed bigot but now as she looked at him she saw the gentle, kind, thinking man. She thought of Luke in Australia; he was taking longer than he thought to sort out his affairs.

She thought how lucky she was to know such men. All of them having so much about them. Whatever happened to them in life they would all be survivors, they would never need her. But how wrong yet again she would be proved.

She gently woke John and told him to go to bed. He woke bleary eyed and began to fall asleep again. She went upstairs and found a blanket and brought it back down. John was sleeping peacefully; he looked so serene. She covered him with the blanket and suddenly felt the urge to kiss him. She gently kissed his cheek and whispered, "Night night, sleep tight, don't worry it will all turn out alright, you'll see," and she went to bed.

Wendy phoned the next day to cancel.

Chapter Twenty-seven

"You must tell him," ordered Lucy.

"I know," said Steph, and so she sat down that dreary Saturday morning and wrote to Luke.

She told him that she didn't love him, that she liked him but that wasn't enough for her. She also said that she didn't feel that she was ready to settle down. She wanted to concentrate on her social work for a while. She said that she was sorry but that she couldn't be dishonest with him. As she wrote, she found that tears swelled up in her eyes.

All the men in her life flashed by and she remembered how she had felt for Steve; she had loved him so much and for so long had pretended to herself that them finishing and him marrying Kate was OK. It wasn't and at times she had thought about trying to win him back. But every time she thought about it she then thought again how ridiculous it would be. No, she had to move on as she did now with Luke.

She also had to put Alan as a no go. He just wasn't interested. He had had several opportunities to be interested in her, but hadn't taken up any of her flirtatious overtures. And John, well, he was like an adopted brother. They felt comfortable with each other and could share lots of things. He certainly had changed, he wasn't that arrogant bigoted man that she had first known but it just didn't seem that he was the man for her.

And then one day she saw him.

She was visiting her dad at the hospital. They had decided to keep him in for a few weeks as on the day that he was due to go home he had suffered another, much more major stroke. This time his speech had been affected and the nurses were much more worried about him. The doctors had some difficulties understanding why he had this stroke and two minor ones a few days later and so there was no plan for him to go home.

Steph had started going to the hospital with her mum. Her course had now finished and she was working part-time at Safeway while she applied for social work jobs. She had planned to apply earlier but when her dad had his stroke she decided that supporting her mum and starting a new job was too much. She still did her few shifts at the Orchard and they had offered her more hours but she thought if she did more she would never leave. John had worked it out that with the money he gave her, the money from the Orchard and a few hours at Safeway she could get by fine and start to pay off some of her student loan (if they lived on baked beans, he had joked).

So, one day, a couple of weeks after her dad had his stroke she had seen him. She hadn't known his name for a while but had commented to her mum how gorgeous he was.

His name was Raj, she had never fallen for an Asian bloke before; there had been a gorgeous-looking Afro-Caribbean bloke on her course but he already had a girlfriend. Of course, she knew nothing about Raj but the day that John went with her to the hospital he said on the way home, "You were flirting rather a lot with that Indian doctor, weren't you Steph?"

She blushed and said, "Was I?" knowing full well that she was. So the day the call came she had no hesitation in saying yes. She had given him her number in case there were problems with her father.

"Hello can I speak to Stephanie please?"

"This is Stephanie," she had replied.

"Hello, this is Raj... the doctor looking after your father. Don't worry he is fine. I just wondered," he said, hesitating, "perhaps this isn't appropriate."

"Sorry?" said Steph.

"I wondered whether you would consider going on a date with me."

Steph felt herself blushing as she said that she would love to go out with Raj.

"Oh... good... I am so pleased," he said.

They talked about the fact that he was her father's doctor but as he wasn't her's and he was only a junior doctor, he didn't feel that it should affect them.

"So you are meeting him tonight?" said Lucy "Are you sure he's not married with three kids?"

"Lucy, why should he be any more married with kids than anyone else?"

"Well, he's a bit old not to be married."

"What, thirty-one years old?" Steph remarked.

"But he is Asian," Lucy said.

Steph realized how prejudiced a lot of her friends were. They seemed much more reserved about her meeting with Raj than they had been with her meeting Luke. She hadn't heard anything from Luke and so assumed that she would never see him again.

She had two jobs to apply for. One of them was in the team where she had done her last placement and so she thought that she better fill the application forms in before she went on the date with Raj.

A few days before, Wendy had announced that she was coming to stay. It sounded like an order and initially Steph felt a bit put out. It was her house after all. But she wanted to support John. He had been getting on well with his book.

"Are you sure you are alright about her coming here?" he had said. Steph had reassured him that it was OK and she had realized that she was quite a good actress and becoming an accomplished liar.

So she went on her first date with Raj. They went for a meal in a Chinese restaurant. Raj said that he loved Chinese food as he had too much Indian food at home. He lived with his parents. He said that when he was sixteen they had tried to sort out an arranged marriage for him but he had said that as he wanted to be a doctor it would be years until he would be ready to marry. When he was twenty-eight he had told his parents that he wanted to choose his own bride. He had been out with Asian women as well as white women and to him it didn't matter what the colour of the person was, that he just had to find the woman that he felt comfortable with and found himself in love with. He said that he had thought that he had found that woman eighteen months before, a fellow doctor who he had fallen madly in love with, but she was just playing him along and eventually married a builder and went to live in Jersey.

Chapter Twenty-eight

"I'm getting on really well with Alan," Paul said. "Can I ring him?"

"OK," Steph replied. She didn't know why, but whenever anyone mentioned Alan's name she felt a tingle go through her body.

Paul seemed so happy these days and even his mum seemed to be getting on better. She had ditched her man, the one who supplied her with drugs, and her social worker was really pleased with her. She had been re-housed several miles from where she used to live and there were plans for two of the children to come and visit more often. She had talked about having Paul back and it was Paul that told her that it just wouldn't work. She had joked to Paul about getting together with Alan but yet again Paul had said that she just wasn't his type.

"He's got some free time this afternoon and so is coming over," said Paul. "I know I was supposed to do some extra work with you, but can't I do it later, please Steph?"

"Well, you get off to school and don't be a pain and I'll think about it" she replied.

"I thought your new social worker was coming to see you today?"

"She is, she can meet Alan too."

Steph had started at 7.30am and was working until 6pm. They were short of staff and when they had asked if she could stay on a bit she had agreed partly because she needed the money but also because Alan was coming.

She was getting on well with Raj and he had talked about her meeting his family. She had only been out with him for a couple of weeks and so was a bit wary.

They had slept together and it was nice but it just wasn't as good as it was with Steve or that brief fling that she had with John before he married Wendy. She thought that nobody could ever beat Steve in the bedroom department but John had and yet now she saw him as her brother so the idea of nookie just seemed slightly repulsive.

She liked Raj a lot; he was fun to be with and was very loving but she wondered whether it was all going a bit too fast. Rather different to Alan; she had fancied him for nearly two years, since she had started her course, and yet she had never passed Go.

"I wonder if I could have a few minutes with Paul on my own?" the new social worker, Cath, said.

"Of course. Alan come into the kitchen with me and I'll make us all a drink."

Steph never said coffee as she didn't like tea or coffee. She had been forced to drink it on occasions but now she had become more forceful in her dislike. People always asked her what she drank instead and she had always been surprised by this and wondered whether half of them had ever been shopping as there was so many alternatives available in the shops. "What about fruit teas?" some had said but to Steph they just tasted like tea dipped in some flavouring. Alan sipped his cup of tea.

"So are you back from the States for good then?" said Steph, munching a chocolate biscuit.

"I'll have to go back to sort out a few things and then I'll be here for good," he replied.

Steph felt herself blushing again. She felt a little uncomfortable in Alan's presence. Alan looked directly at her and said, "I am serious about taking Paul on. I really like him."

"But what if you find a woman who doesn't like him? What would you do then?"

"I just wouldn't be interested in her. Besides, there is already someone I like and she really likes Paul."

Steph felt her cheeks burning.

"But the trouble is that she is going out with someone else. I have known her for quite some time now and have just not had the courage to ask her out... she is so much better a person than I am."

Paul and Cath came into the room.

"Alan, it's all sorted," he said, running up to Alan. "They say that they will support you being my dad, and mum has agreed... and..."

"Hold on, Paul, there is a long way to go yet."

"But Cath, you said."

"Yes Paul, but..."

"It's because I'm on my own, isn't it?" said Alan. "They want me to be married."

"Well marry Steph," said Paul. "She can ditch her new bloke and besides you've always fancied each other."

"Paul," said Cath, looking sternly at him.

But Steph knew that those words were so true, she had always fancied Alan and surely the woman that he was talking about had to be her. Alan looked at her in a way that she just hadn't seen before; suddenly she felt a tremendous rush and she knew that it was Alan that she wanted.

Chapter Twenty-nine

"John, stop getting in such a flap."

"I can't help it. I haven't seen her for five months and I just don't know…"

"Of course you don't know… come here."

Steph pulled John towards her, put her arms around him and held him tightly.

"I'll be here… just don't worry," she said assertively, suddenly feeling very protective towards John.

"But…"

She held him more tightly and then suddenly she felt him relax. The door bell rang.

"Its her… she's here," he said tightening in her arms.

"I'll go."

Steph let go of John and gave him a gentle reassuring kiss on his cheek. She went to the front door and standing on the doorstep surrounded by bags was Luke.

"Hi," he said, throwing his arms around Steph.

"Didn't you get my letter?" she said

"Yes, aren't you going to let me in?"

Steph let him pass her and enter the house. John was in the hallway.

"Hi Luke," he said.

The phone rang and Steph went to answer it.

"Hi Steph, is John there?"

"Yes, hold on I'll get him for you."

She handed the phone to John and mouthed the word "Wendy". Luke, meanwhile, was bringing his bags into the hall. "Well, aren't you gonna make me a cuppa?" he said.

"Oh yes, of course, come into the kitchen."

"Steph, I know what you wrote. But you never know what the future can bring and so don't just write me off in your life."

Luke looked very serious and went to put his arms around Steph but she pulled away.

"You are right Luke, you don't know what the future will bring. I never expected to not be with Steve but things happen and that's just the way things are. I told you that I felt that I didn't want to settle with anyone and, in fact, I have a new boyfriend. I just had to be honest with you."

"I've got nowhere to stay," he said. "Can I stay here for a few days until I get myself sorted?"

Steph hesitated in her reply; she knew that Wendy would be coming to stay and she didn't know whether she would be sleeping in with John. In fact, she hoped that she wouldn't be. She didn't want him to be pulled back to the life that he led before.

"You can sleep on my floor," she said.

"OK," he said and then she began to regret it. She wondered what Raj would say and whether Luke would try it on, but she felt sorry for him.

"Can I have a bath?" Luke asked.

"Of course you can, get yourself a towel out of the airing cupboard."

"Wendy will be here in a couple of hours," said John.

"Stop panicking," Steph said, putting her arms around John.

She seemed to give him a lot of reassuring cuddles these days and he would just relax in her arms.

"So what's happening with Luke?"

She told John what they had said and John looked worried.

"Oh don't worry, it will be fine," she said. But she wasn't convincing. She realized that she just didn't really know Luke at all.

"And what will you tell Raj?"

"I'm not sure… It's a good job that I am not seeing him for a few days."

Chapter Thirty

"Hi Steph." Alan was getting out of his car just as she walked past it. She hadn't noticed him parked there. She never expected to find him at the local Safeway.

"I'm living around the corner from you," he said. "I found a small house to rent because my house still has a tenant and, besides, I'm not sure that I want to go back there. Perhaps we could have a coffee after we have finished our shopping; what do you think?"

"OK, I've got quite a lot of shopping to do though," said Steph.

She realized that she was trying to put him off a bit, but then thought, what's wrong with a friendly coffee and coke.

"I'm not in any hurry," he said.

She found herself hurrying around the shop; suddenly it was important to get to the cafe to make sure that she didn't lose him yet again. She always seemed to be losing him but this time surely he wouldn't run away from her.

She was working at the Orchard that afternoon but she still had a couple of hours, time enough to get home and put away the shopping and yet time for Alan too.

She went up the aisle with the toilet rolls and suddenly found herself face to face with Raj. He was pushing a trolley with a baby and a toddler sitting in it. He seemed to try to ignore her, which she thought was strange, and then an Asian woman appeared. "Give Daddy a piece," she said to the child, who was eating a Kit Kat.

Raj looked at Steph in a pleading way as if to say please don't tell. Steph looked away and walked past. She felt stunned, shocked, bewildered but strangely relieved.

"Are you OK?" said Alan. "Yes... well, actually no," she said.

They sat silently sharing their drinks and then Steph said that she had better go home to get ready to go to work. Alan walked with her to the car. She got in, started the engine and found tears running down her face. She cried all the way home. She had been duped again. Why did this keep happening to her. When would she find the honest, true man? These were all questions flooding through her head. How could he shop where she shopped with his wife and children? It just seemed so crazy.

She parked the car, opened the front door and headed for her bedroom. She thought that she would lie down for half an hour before she got ready to go to work. She opened the door and there, lying on her bed, obviously in the middle of sexual passions were two people who she quickly identified as Luke and Wendy.

"Excuse me," she said, shutting the door behind her.

She went to look for John. He was out in the garage.

"Did you know that your wife was humping my ex?" she said in a cold manner.

"Oh," said John.

"I'm sorry, I shouldn't have said it like that," she said.

He had been mending a puncture on his bike and marched past Steph brushing her slightly. She heard his voice shouting, "Get out, the pair of you."

There was a load of commotion and then Steph heard the front door close and sobbing coming from the hallway. Steph found John sitting on the floor curled up in the hall crying. She knelt down and put her arms around him.

"I think I really loved her, Steph," he said.

"No, you didn't, you are just hurt, that's all."

That night it seemed very quiet with only the two of them. Wendy and Luke were both bubbly characters and although it hadn't been ideal the four of them had had a laugh together. It was their indiscretion that had got to both John and Steph. How could they do it so openly?

"But at least now it's final," John remarked. "If she had really wanted me she wouldn't have jumped into bed with Luke after a few days, would she Steph?"

"No, she wouldn't."

Steph hadn't told John about meeting Alan and bumping into Raj; such a lot had seemed to have happened during the past week. When Wendy arrived Steph had wondered whether perhaps John would get back with her. Wendy had been such fun to be with and she found herself being enchanted by her but when John went to sleep on the settee and let her have his bedroom she thought that perhaps she would never get rid of her.

Luke had made some overtures to her both the first and second night but she had resisted his charm and had no regrets. She had thought that she would make a go of it with Raj.

He had called to arrange to meet her and had been very understanding about the whole situation. She had thought that she must push Alan out of her mind altogether and settle with Raj. Now she was in turmoil once again.

After work she rang Lucy and told her everything.

"Blimey," said Lucy, "your life is like a soap opera. You've only got to have Steve turn up and declare his everlasting, undying love for you and well, you'd have nearly everything."

Lucy always managed to cheer Steph up. She had done really well in the first year of her course and was really looking forward to the second year.

"By the way Tom's got a job."

"Where?"

"In the same office where you were on placement but in the short-term team. He starts on Monday. Have you heard anything yet from your application, that was weeks ago wasn't it?"

"Yes, I assume that they don't want me. Life's so hectic at the mo anyhow that I'm not sure that I could handle it."

Steph had a lovely soak in the bath. She used some bubble bath that Luke had given her. It smelt nice and she didn't blame him. She just felt sad for John.

She went into the kitchen and John said that Alan had rung while she was in the bath.

"He said that he would ring back in half an hour; that was about ten minutes ago, I suppose."

Steph felt panicky. She wondered what Alan was ringing about. She wanted him to ring but didn't at the same time.

Chapter Thirty-one

"I'm going shopping; we need some toilet rolls and there is no bog cleaner. Do you want me to get you anything? By the way an old colleague of mine rang me earlier today, he is now working at the Beeb and wondered if I might be interested in a bit of work. He was a bit vague though... you're not listening to me Steph, are you?"

"Sorry," Steph replied, "you asked if I wanted anything from the shops."

"Oh, never mind," said John, who was a bit put out by Steph's lack of interest.

He sometimes felt that they were like an old married couple who got on well at times and then at other's weren't even aware of the other's existence. He, however, increasingly found himself very interested in anything that Steph had to say and he rarely drank coffee these days and could easily join her orange squash society.

Yes, there was something about Steph. The day that she had put her arms around him when Wendy was caught in bed with Luke he had been so glad that she was there. In fact, he really didn't want to move anywhere else because he just liked being near her and he liked the way that she would twist her upper lip when she got angry about something and twiddle a piece of hair while she watched the TV.

When he had first known Steph it had been just for a laugh. She was so naive. She had been with the same bloke for years. He thought that it would be fun with someone who was training to be a social worker, what a hoot. She would earn peanuts, of course, and he had been out with some women who had mega bucks but after a couple of dates the sex would be stale and they would be expecting the old wedding ring.

It had been a thrill with Steph; she had been so fresh, so uncertain but she had also stood up to him. She believed passionately in what she was doing and he had begun to realize how shallow his life had become. He had thought that if he had a wife perhaps he would be taken more seriously and was surprised to be turned down by so many women. He had always been told that he would be a good catch for someone. He had convinced himself that Wendy was, in fact, the right one. A cousin had once dabbled in numerology and had told him that number six should have some significant meaning to him and so when Wendy accepted as the sixth woman he had asked he convinced himself that she was the one.

Only two weeks after they were married she admitted to spending the night before their wedding with a colleague of his, a rather unsavoury character, and for the next few weeks he had to pass this guy's desk knowing that he was smirking at him.

Steph had always been honest with him and so when he could stand it no longer he knew that she wouldn't turn him away and she hadn't. He knew that he could live in her house for as long as he liked.

He had said that he was writing a novel but for weeks he had been staring at a blank page or just tinkering with some ideas. He had taken to reading Jane Austen books. Steph had been amused, by this, but he was intrigued by the way that she wrote about her society. He had also become intrigued by the woman herself and had decided to join the local Jane Austen society. He had been along to a talk and tried to hide away discretely. He didn't want to let people know that he had been a top London journalist and so had said that he was between jobs.

He enjoyed working in the supermarket and appreciated the wage he earned much more than he had his previous large salary. He always paid Steph her rent but she didn't ask for much. He still had some savings but he was pleased that he managed to live on the small amount that he earnt.

"Why are you staring at me in that way?" Steph had said one night as they watched TV.

John had never really watched much TV but he enjoyed sitting with Steph with a cup of hot chocolate with the gas fire on watching some mindless programme.

"No reason," he said.

"You are doing it again," Steph said in an irritated tone.

"I just thought how much you look like Jane Austen," he said.

"Oh John, don't be daft, I look nothing like her. Besides, how do they know what she actually looks like?"

"There is a picture that one of her relatives drew of her; I've forgotten who it was but they reckon that it's quite a good likeness."

"You'll be joining the Jane Austen society next and going along with all the old maids," she laughed.

"I joined weeks ago," he said, "and, well, its not what I thought, its very interesting."

"So you will write an adaption of *Pride and Prejudice* will you?" she joked.

"No, I think I'd rather do *Persuasion*, I'll be Captain Wentworth and you can be the woman in it, I've forgotten her name."

"It's Anne," said David, a neighbour who popped around from time to time just for a chat.

"So you are a Jane Austen fan too are you?" Steph said.

"No Ian is. Oh, he just loves them when they come on TV and we have all the videos but he's not knowledgeable like John is. Oh, I do like the costumes though," he remarked. "I often thought it would be nice to be a woman during those days, heaving your bosoms at everyone."

David always made them laugh. He lived with his partner, Ian, a few doors away and would often pop around for some comfort when he had a row with Ian.

They were a very interesting pair as David was a solicitor and was a tiny fellow and his partner Ian was a big man who worked as a brickie. Ian had a couple of kids who were in their late teens who would come to stay. Sometimes they would bring them around and they would all share a Chinese. David adored them coming and would fuss around. The younger one, Jenny, had long blond hair. She was thirteen and at the stage of messing with her hair; she brought huge bags of make-up with her. David would often appear looking like a pantomime dame, much to the delight of Jenny.

Stephen, her older brother who was nearly fifteen, was much more conscious of his dad's situation. He had known David for most of his life but was embarrassed by his manner.

"So when are the kids over next?" said Steph.

"Jenny's coming at the weekend but I'm not sure when Stevie's coming again. I'm afraid that he is embarrassed by his dad being an old poof and, well, I just can't give him a cuddle any more. He has a girlfriend now, you know Steph, but he won't bring her around to visit. Ian has talked to Sally and Matt about it but they have said that it is up to Stevie. Oh dear, I must stop calling him Stevie, he told me that I must now call him Steve but after all this time it is so hard."

After David left, Steph and John talked about the situation. It seemed that Ian and his ex-wife and her second husband got on extremely well. Ian had still been living with her when he fell for David and, in fact, it was her that suggested that the only sensible thing to do was for him to "come out". A couple of years later she had met Matt who, coincidentally, had a brother who was gay and so for a number of years the four of them had been able to share the children. In fact Steph had thought that they had over compensated and that the children were rather spoilt. Matt had no children of his own and Sally was unable to have any more and so all four had doted on the two children.

John thought about how loved these two children were compared to many of the children who Steph talked about who turned up at the Orchard. The government for years had advocated children being looked after by foster carers but who would want to be a foster carer and look after a kid who was off the wall. Until John had met Steph he had not really had any contact with this world. Of course he knew that there were kids living with foster parents but he hadn't met anyone who either worked with them or who was a foster parent. David and Ian had thought about being foster parents.

"You would be great," Steph had told them but she and they knew that lots of people would be against them taking on the role just because they were gay, and what would the kids think? Jenny might be OK although Matt had thought that she would be jealous but Steve would find it hard so they had decided against it. Instead, they had decided to become befrienders, which meant going through an assessment process to be approved to have an adult with a learning disability visiting them for a day a week. They were currently being assessed and one day John had popped around when the social worker was there.

"What was she like?" said Steph.

"Quite picky and nosy I thought," said John.

"What do you mean?"

"Well, she asked them all about their sleeping arrangements, such as whether they wore pyjamas or slept in the nude. Do you know, Steph, that she even asked them to turn the TV off."

"Well what's wrong with that? It's really hard trying to talk to someone seriously when they have the telly on. I used to have it all the time when I was on placement."

John often had discussions with Steph about social work. As with Jane Austen, he was finding it more and more interesting and had begun to try to write about it.

As he walked around the shop and put items into the trolley he thought about his life. He often did this and wondered where he was going. He put the toilet rolls in the trolley and was just turning the corner for the toilet cleaner aisle when he witnessed a young woman with a baby shove some baby wipes into her pocket. She looked rather scruffily dressed and the baby looked rather pale. A few minutes later a security man came charging towards them and asked the woman to empty her pockets. Her head was bowed low as she removed the wipes. He heard her say that her child had a sore bottom and so she needed the wipes but couldn't afford them. She was sorry and could he let her off this time.

John carried on doing the shopping and got to the checkout. In front of him was a woman who looked a very similar age to the young woman with the baby. She was with a man who appeared to be her husband and they had a huge trolley full of goodies including several bottles of spirit. He wondered what had happened to the young woman who seemed so desperate she would probably never dream of what this couple had bought.

John noticed that their shopping totalled to over a hundred pounds and that a high proportion of it was luxury items.

He returned home and found Steph stretched out on the settee in her dressing gown, dozing through a film.

"Hello," she said sleepily.

"Did Alan phone?" he said.

"Yes," she replied.

John wanted to tell Steph about the incident in the supermarket but it just didn't seem the right time. Instead, he left her dozing and watching the film and went to his room and his laptop to start writing about it. At last he was burning with ideas. He, like Jane Austen, would write about the people he knew and the people he came across and he would start with the young woman in the supermarket.

Chapter Thirty-two

Steph woke up feeling perky. She had had a lovely chat with Alan the night before and they had agreed to meet that night. They would go out for a meal and then go to the theatre afterwards.

She went into the kitchen and saw John standing in his underpants, hovering by the back door.

"Shut the door, it's freezing and you make me feel even colder standing there like that. Go and put some clothes on."

"OK Mum," John grinned.

"The post has arrived and there's an important one here for you." Steph picked up her letters.

John often wandered around with hardly anything on and she had commented on it from time to time as she thought that some of her friends were a bit more prudish than she was but John never took any notice.

Lucy had told her not to get so freaked out about it.

"Just enjoy the view," she had said.

Yes, John did have a nice body and he didn't flaunt it particularly. She had said to him once that he should join a naturist group but he said, "But then you'd see my willy every morning and you might not fancy the view at that time of day." She'd never really contemplated the view at any time. John was like a brother to her and the idea of having anything to do with his body seemed rather incestuous.

"I don't think I'd turn him down if he offered himself to me," Lucy had said.

"But what would Tom feel?" she had replied.

"Oh Steph, chill out, don't take things so seriously," Lucy remarked. "It's never likely to happen anyhow; why on earth would someone like John be interested in me. Come on, get real."

Steph didn't really understand what she meant.

Steph opened the brown envelope and found a single sheet of paper. She read the letter.

"Well?" said John.

"Well what?" said Steph.

"Is it an interview or not?"

"Yes, its on 22nd."

"Well, that's a good luck omen. Isn't it?"

John knew that for some reason Steph had this strange idea that 2s and 7s were lucky. Some days he had thought that he was surrounded by these nutty women who were either into weird and wonderful diets, synchronicity or psychic phenomena. Nearly every women he knew could see a coincidence in everything.

But the strange thing was that it was rubbing off on him too. Every time that Steph went to a car park someone she had stood next to in the checkout queue would get into the car next to hers when she started to load her shopping. The last few times John had been shopping it had happened to him too.

"Oh that's good that'll give you a week to lose that stone of weight that you are always on about," John said, with a grin all over his face.

"You cheeky sod," Steph said, pulling a face back and sticking her tongue out at him.

Chapter Thirty-three

It was 5.30pm and Alan was picking her up at six. They had decided to go to the local pizza bar as the show started at 7.30pm and so they needed somewhere where they would get served quickly.

"Steph that's about the fifth time that you've been to the toilet in the last half hour," John said "just calm down."

He came over, pulled Steph to him and tickled her.

"Get off," she said.

"By the way, you seem to be writing a lot at the moment. Can I read it?"

"Soon," he said.

"You are being very mysterious."

"No, I just want to get it right, that's all."

"By the way," said Steph, "what happened to your friend coming to stay... you know, that bloke that started working at the Beeb."

"I'm not sure," said John, "I'll have to give him a ring."

The door bell rang and John went to open it. "Off you go for your last wee," he said smiling.

John opened the door and invited Alan to come in. He suddenly felt rather strange; he knew that Steph had liked Alan for ages. He was pleased for her that at last she had got to go out with him but he suddenly felt a pang of jealousy.

"Have a good time," he said as he shut the door behind them.

"We will," Alan replied.

John went back to his room and suddenly the house seemed very quiet. He decided to read aloud his latest writing. He was a better judge of its quality if he read aloud.

The phone rang and it was his friend, the one who worked for the Beeb. He chatted to him for a while and they agreed a date for him to come and stay. He would sleep on the settee and let his friend have his bed.

John thought that perhaps there was something in synchronicity and coincidences and he was still convinced that Steph looked like Jane Austen. Steph was a little plumper but her face and eyes were very similar to the picture in the book that he had borrowed from the library.

Perhaps Steph was a reincarnation of Jane, he mused, but if that was the case why didn't she want to write?

Chapter Thirty-four

Steph couldn't believe that she was actually going out with Alan. She had dreamt of this day for so long. She knew that she had fancied Alan from the very first time that she had seen him at university and now it was two years on. So much seemed to have happened in that time. She didn't regret her time with Luke or with Raj. She had learnt a lot from both experiences but throughout that experience she had still felt bewitched by Alan. Every time that she heard his name it had sent a shiver down her spine and now here she was sitting close to him sharing a pizza. It tasted like the best pizza that she had ever had in her life and the glass of wine that she was sipping made her feel slightly tipsy.

"Do you want a pudding?" he said

"I think I'd rather have an ice cream in the interval at the theatre," she replied.

The play wasn't particularly good but Steph just liked being there sitting next to Alan. She wanted to touch his hand or his arm but didn't. He didn't touch her either and she found herself burning inside.

"Are you alright?" Alan said in the interval as they sipped their drinks.

"Yes, I'm fine. It's just a bit hot in here," she said.

The second half was even slower and Steph found herself dozing and had to shake herself a couple of times to wake up. As they walked out of the theatre Alan took her hand and said, "I must admit that I was bored for most of the play and had great difficulty staying awake with the heat. What did you think?"

She laughed and said that she felt exactly the same.

Alan continued holding her hand as she walked to the car. They drove back to Steph's house and as they reached her road. Steph asked if Alan wanted to come in for a drink.

"That would be nice," Alan replied.

"Well?" said John as he hovered next to Steph. "Well, how did you get on then?"

"The play was boring," Steph said, "and I had great difficulty staying awake."

"But what about the company?"

"Oh, he's lovely but I feel a little nervous."

"But that's not surprising, you've been dying to go out with him for so long."

Steph took the drinks into the living room, a coffee for Alan and an orange juice for herself.

"Sorry I was so long," she said, "our kettle takes ages to boil."

She realized after she said that the words she should have said "my" but she was so used to having John around that it just seemed natural to say "our". For a second she wondered if she was doing the right thing but then John walked in said he was going to bed and left. Steph looked across at Alan and thought, yes, I truly fancy this man. They sipped their drinks and chatted about all sorts of things and then Steph asked how the adoption of Paul was going.

"Fine," said Alan. "We hope that the whole process will be completed before the end of the year."

Throughout the conversation they had sat on separate seats and Alan prepared himself to go.

"I've had a lovely evening Steph, even though the play was awful," he laughed. "I'd really like to meet up again soon, that's if you'd like that."

"Yes, that would be nice," Steph replied.

Chapter Thirty-five

"Do I look OK?"

"You look fine," John said.

Steph was going to her interview. She had looked on the internet for any change in current practices and had spoken to Tom about things too. It seemed ages since she had been in the team.

"Time for you to go," John said, pushing Steph towards the door.

"Are you sure I look OK?" she said.

"Yes," said John, this time sounding a little irritated.

She had tried on five lots of clothes and had left the others all in a pile on her bed to sort out later. She just felt so nervous and wanted to give up and go back to her old job. The job that she had done for so many years. She wanted to be with Steve, she wanted it to be just like it was two years before.

But then she knew that really she didn't want it to be like that at all. She wanted to be a social worker but she was just so scared.

"You go to the interview for me," she said to John in a childlike voice.

"Go now," ordered John, pushing her out of the door. "I'll be here to celebrate or cry with you when you get back."

That made Steph feel good, knowing that John would be there.

"Are you sure I look…" she couldn't get the last words out as John pushed her out and shut the door behind her.

John stood in the corridor and found that just for a few seconds he couldn't move. It suddenly came to him how much he loved the woman that he had pushed out of the door but she thought of him like a brother. That certainly wasn't the way that he felt about her. He went into the kitchen and put the kettle on and then felt he needed a pee and so went upstairs to the toilet. Afterwards he passed Steph's room and saw that the door was ajar. Lying in a disorganized muddle on the bed were Steph's discarded clothes. He went in and found himself sitting amongst her clothes, touching them, smelling them.

The phone rang and he found himself jolted out of his trance-like state. He darted downstairs and picked it up.

"Oh, hi," he said.

"I liked what you wrote. Have you thought about my offer?"

"I'm not sure," said John.

"Well, I need a decision soon and I think you'd be a fool not to take this opportunity."

John thought about how he felt about Steph and suddenly it was all crystal clear. He had to take the job. He had to move to Manchester. He needed to return to his roots and this opportunity would never come again. The chance to work both for a newspaper, do some TV work and still have time to write his novel.

"Yes, I'll come," he said.

Chapter Thirty-six

"Stephanie, we would like to ask you a few questions. We ask the same questions to all of our candidates. Is that OK with you?"

Steph was too nervous to say no but she thought about it afterwards. Tom had told her what the interviewing process was like and that usually there would be some questions about social work law and that there was always one about anti-oppressive practice.

While on placement Steph had worked with a very experienced agency worker, Clare, who had decided to give up her permanent post to work casually through an agency. This was because she had youngish children who just wanted their mum around during the summer holidays. Steph had found her views very interesting and her passion for social work and the rights of service users. She said that it was easier as an agency worker to be loyal to service users and not get trapped in all of the bureaucratic systems. They had discussed all the changes that had happened since Clare had become a social worker. She agreed that some were beneficial but others had just lead to an increasing amount of bureaucracy.

Clare said that when she made herself available for a job she generally just met the team manager and had a chat and yet if she applied formally she would have to go through the equal opportunities process that she questioned. She had proven time and time again that she was good at her job and that she treated her service users with respect. She felt that everyone that she worked with had individual needs but that often she was forced into treating them as types.

Steph thought about this as she sat drinking a hot chocolate. She had answered the questions the best way that she could but she was fearful of saying her true feelings. Tom had warned her off.

"They don't really want to know the truth," he had said, "they can't handle it. You just have to tell them what they want to hear and then when you have the job you can stand up for what you believe."

She remembered this discussion. It was soon after she had found out about Raj and his secret family. She had wondered at the time all about lies and the truth. She thought about the discussions at uni about being open and honest. Her mum would have said that a white lie didn't hurt but she couldn't even use this terminology at uni.

Her black friend Jacqui, whose mum came from Jamaica to the UK when she was ten years old, laughed when Steph told her about not being able to say a white lie. "Its just ridiculous" she said sarcastically, "that's really going to stop white people treating black people as if they are idiots."

Steph finished her drink and headed back home.

"How did it go?" said John.

"I'm not sure, I was so nervous," Steph replied.

"Oh well it's only your first interview so it doesn't really matter one way or the other."

John decided not to tell Steph about moving to Manchester. He wasn't leaving for a few weeks and so today was not the day to tell her

.

"I love you Steph," said Alan. "I think that I always have." He put his arms around Steph. They had been to the theatre again and this time had seen *Annie* and giggled through it. They were so much closer and held hands through the whole of the performance. Steph felt comfortable and happy but not contented.

"What's the matter?" said Alan

"Oh nothing," Steph replied, "I was just thinking about my job interview."

"Leave it for now, you can't do anything about it," Alan said, kissing her on the neck. "Do you want to come back to my place?" he said.

"OK," she said "I'll just phone John and tell him."

"Why bother? He knows that you are with me. He'll assume that you've come home with me."

"OK."

She wondered why she felt uncomfortable with not phoning John, but she did.

John fell asleep watching the late movie. He had stayed up just because he wasn't ready to go to bed. He had chatted to a few women online. He had joined a dating site but hadn't told Steph as he wasn't sure how she would react. He thought that she would make fun of him. Recently he had lost interest in dating anyone and just enjoyed watching TV with Steph, sharing a crumpet or a cheese toastie.

When it was crumpets Steph seemed to make them but it was he who seemed always to make the cheese toasties. Steph said that it was because she was frightened of breaking daisy's head. They had a toastie-maker which was shaped like a cow and on the packaging was called Daisy. John had given it to Steph as a present when he got some money for writing an article for a magazine.

He went to bed wondering why Steph hadn't called but he knew that she was staying at Alan's house.

"I really do love you Steph," said Alan.

"I know and I love you too," she said but she thought that she didn't sound very convincing.

"I know that this might be the wrong time and you know that I'm not really good at romantic things but well... I want to marry you... will you?" he said in a pleading voice.

"Yes," she said but yet again she thought that she didn't sound very convincing.

"Oh, that's brilliant" he said.

Chapter Thirty-seven

"That's brilliant," said Lucy. "What did John say?"

"I haven't told him yet."

"I expect he will be pleased for you but sad also."

"Why?"

"Oh come on Steph, you know that he loves you."

"Yes, but like a sister."

"You are always so idealistic. Don't you forget that you got into bed with him and how you admitted to me how good it was?"

"Yes, that was ages ago and you know that I have always fancied Alan ever since I first saw him at uni."

Steph listened to her own voice. Was she trying to convince herself? Was it really the game that she liked, attracting the man, rather than the idea of settling down with him? No, she said to herself, she really loved Alan; but doubts kept creeping into her mind.

John's friend Pete came to stay and Steph had a shock because she had visions of a not so good looking man for some reason but he turned out to be gorgeous but gay.

Alan was reassured. "I don't want anyone taking you from me, my love," he said after the first time that he met Pete.

Pete was in between assignments and so he was to stay with Steph and John for two weeks.

"Have you told her yet?" Steph overheard Pete saying to John, the second morning when she came down for breakfast.

"What haven't you told me?" Steph exclaimed as she walked into the kitchen in her dressing gown.

"Oh nothing," said John, who seemed rather embarrassed.

"When do you start your job?" Pete asked.

"Next Monday," Steph replied. "It's my last day working at the Orchard today... It's strange... I shall miss it."

"But you will still have Paul."

"Yes."

"Who's Paul?" said Pete.

"He's Steph's fiancé's adoptive child, who used to live at the Orchard."

"Coo er, you don't 'alf live a complicated life," Pete said.

John thought about his life over the last year or so and how much it had changed. Pete said that he was different, much calmer, less fractious. He felt that Steph had been a good influence on John and he was happy that he had such a good friend, a friend that he should keep for always.

They had talked about him moving to Manchester and the projects that he was to be involved with. One included a new TV series which was about a social work team. John was writing six pilot episodes, the studio, although wary, were also excited about his story-lines. Steph had been so busy in her own world and so John had not shared them with her but the main character was based on Steph. Besides, he didn't feel confident enough to read it to her. He suddenly realized that his outward confidence was all a sham and that in many ways he was shy, not reserved but shy.

Steph wondered what the news was that John had to tell her. She asked Alan what he thought it was.

"I expect that it's his book," he said.

"I suppose so," she replied.

"Oh Ian's just impossible."

"What's he done now?" said Steph as she put the washing in the washing machine. She went in John's jeans trouser pockets and found a piece of paper folded up.

"Oh, a secret love letter," David exclaimed in a suddenly perky voice.

"Give it here," and he snatched it off her, opened the paper and began to read quicker than Steph could say anything. "Oh dear."

"What?" said Steph.

"Our John is leaving us."

"What do you mean?" Steph said in a worried tone

"Here, read this."

Steph read the note it was from a TV studio in Manchester and said that they were looking forward to working closely with John when he moved to Manchester.

Chapter Thirty-eight

"When were you going to tell me?" Steph said.

"I don't know," John replied, looking away from her.

"Steph, stop making such a big deal about it," said Alan, putting his arms around her. She released herself and moved away from Alan and looked directly at John again.

"I'm sorry," John said. "I just kind of couldn't tell you, that's all."

"So when will you be moving then?" Alan said.

"In ten days' time," John replied.

"Don't worry, I won't leave you in the lurch."

"It's not the money," Steph said, "it's..."

Pete walked in and asked if anyone fancied going for a walk. "I will," said David. He had been around a lot since Pete had arrived and had invited himself to tea the night before.

Steph had asked him whether Ian wanted to come as well but as it was half term he was spending some time with the kids. David had suggested to Ian that he took them to the pictures. Alan reckoned that it was a ploy so that he could come over.

"He really fancies Pete, you know Steph."

"No you're wrong, he loves Ian."

"I know that he does, but that doesn't stop him fancying someone else."

They had this great discussion about whether you could really fancy someone if you were truly in love with someone else. Alan felt that you could still fancy other people whereas Steph said that she felt that you couldn't. As she said this she wondered what it was that she really felt for John. She knew now that she loved Alan and was certain that she wanted to spend her life with him but she also realized that there was much more than a brother/sister attraction to John.

"Did you have a nice walk?" said Alan.

"Oh lovely," said David standing rather too close to Pete.

"I was wondering, Steph," said Pete, "whether I could become your weekend lodger, I'd pay you the monthly rate, of course, but for the present my job would keep me in London."

"I'll think about it," said Steph.

"What's your problem?" said Alan. "You'd be able to keep the money and…"

"I don't know. There is just something about him… besides some of his views are so outlandish."

"If it didn't work you could always chuck him out."

Steph decided to sit in the garden and think about it. Alan said that he'd get the tea. He was a good cook, like Steve, but very different to Steve as a person. As she sat in the garden a robin came over and sat near to her. She asked the robin what she should do and he chirped back at her a jolly sound. She thought that he was telling her to give Pete a chance.

"Hello, you're in a world of your own. I'll go and leave you to it." John started walking away but Steph grabbed the sleeve of his jumper.

"No stay, keep me company," she said.

"OK."

They sat looking at the clouds in the sky and played the game that they had often played about what words and pictures they could see. John was the only person who could see what she could see. Alan tried hard to see but he couldn't; she reckoned that it was something to do with what they did as a job but then the law was full of words too.

"Oh, look at that," she said, "it looks just like Donald Duck."

"So it does," said John.

"I'm going to miss this when you've gone," Steph said, "in fact I'm really gonna miss you, John."

"And I will miss you too, but you have Alan now and you've always had Alan. It has been great here being with you and I have learnt a lot but I have to live my own life now and it's not about picking up the pieces, it's about starting afresh."

John put his arms around Steph and she began to cry.

"Steph, don't cry. I know we've been very close but I have to go."

"I know," she said and wiped tears away. She felt so comfortable in his arms. Could it be that she was in love with two men? They walked in the house together and Steph felt guilty, as if she was having an illicit affair.

"I'm gonna miss looking at the clouds with Steph," John said to Alan as he opened a bottle of wine.

"Yes, it's strange how you can both see the same patterns, I try but I just can't see them. I really love Steph, you know, John. When I went to the States I thought about her a lot of the time. I was a fool not to have told her earlier but now I am so happy."

"And Paul, does he know yet that you are going to marry?"

"Yes, I told him at the weekend and he is over the moon. Of course, it makes a slight difference to the adoption but the social worker tells me that it shouldn't be a problem."

"And what about babies? You know Steph would like kids."

"And so would I."

"What are you two intensely talking about?" said Steph, as she came into the kitchen.

"Oh just you, me, clouds and things," said Alan as he kissed her on the cheek.

"What things?" said Steph suspiciously.

"Babies," said John.

"Oh, I see. Give me a chance, I start a new job tomorrow and you talk about babies!"

John and Alan just laughed.

The rest of the evening flew by. David flirted atrociously with Pete and Pete seemed to love it. Steph was too busy in her own world to notice, she stopped worrying about the two men in her life and started worrying about starting the job. She worried about whether she could do it and so she drank very little. Alan had wanted to stay the night but Steph felt that she needed to be alone for a few nights until she had been in her job a few days. Alan understood, he always understood and, in fact, Paul was staying over for a few days and he wanted to concentrate on him.

"When Paul is with you permanently can I be you babysitter?" David said.

"That will depend on Paul," Alan said.

"Is that because I'm gay?"

"No, it's because Paul has to choose who he would like."

Steph was surprised at Alan's attitude and as he got up to go she said, "It is because he's gay, isn't it?"

"Not exactly. Its because of the way he is flirting with Pete; he's like a time bomb."

"What do you mean?"

"Oh come on Steph, you mean that you didn't see it?"

Chapter Thirty-nine

Steph woke early and decided to get up and have a long soak in the bath.

The discussions of the night before were now behind her. What mattered was doing a good job. She was now going to practice as a qualified social worker and ringing in her head was what John had said when she went to bed.

"Just think what adventures you will have."

She hadn't really seen them that way but she thought that perhaps that's the way they would seem through the eyes of a writer. John had told her that he was writing a trial TV series around a team of social workers and that he expected Steph to be his consultant.

"And how much will I get paid?" she had said.

"Oh, with my everlasting gratitude," he grinned.

"And love as well," she added.

"Oh, that goes without saying, I will always love you Stephanie Clover," he said saluting her.

She soaked in the bath and the last three years drifted through her mind. What a time it had been. Losing Steve, longing for Alan, brief flings with Raj and Luke and her attitude changing completely about John. They weren't really like the characters in *Pride and Prejudice* as he just wasn't proud. But she had certainly been prejudiced about him. She had been charmed by him but also repulsed by his lifestyle and attitudes but now it was as if she knew a totally different man. She wondered what he would be like when he went to Manchester. They had agreed to meet up regularly but she knew that it wouldn't be that often as she wanted her time with Alan, needed to take on her two new roles, as social worker and mother to Paul.

The water began to get cold and so she pulled out the plug and had a top up. She remembered what her nanna had said when she was a teenager about turning into a prune and laughed silently. She missed Nanna and when her dad was in hospital she began to panic that she would lose him too but he had made a full recovery.

She heard the alarm go off in her bedroom. She had forgotten to turn it off. A couple of minutes later she heard John's voice

"Are you up Steph?"

"I'm in the bath," she shouted.

"Hi Steph, good to have you back," said Martin. "I've got some cases lined up for you but before you get involved with them you need to attend some of the induction meetings."

He handed her a two-week programme.

"Where's Clive?" Steph asked Sarah. "Oh, he's left, didn't you know?"

"No."

"Well, he and Martin had a major row so he decided to leave. I think he's doing agency work at the moment."

Steph knew that Sarah was hiding something and, later in the day, she asked Dennis what had happened.

"You know what Clive was like; well his lack of recording caught up with him when the inspectors were in and that lead to the row."

"Oh, I see."

"How did it go?" said Alan over the phone. Steph had asked Alan to just be in touch by phone for a couple of days until she knew what she was doing.

"OK, well, a bit boring really. I have to do this induction programme and I really just want to get on with some proper work... Oh and Clive's gone. It seems like there was some bust up between him and Martin, the team manager."

"Good stories for John then."

"I suppose, but I haven't seem him yet this evening, he wasn't here when I got home."

Steph watched the TV and went to bed. She dozed off and then awoke suddenly.

"What are you doing?" Steph said, as she saw John hovering at her doorway.

"I was just looking at you," he said

"Are you drunk?"

"Nope. How did your first day go?"

"Fine, but you weren't here when I got home to tell you all about it."

"Sorry, I had a date."

"Who with?" Steph suddenly felt uncomfortable and a little jealous. It hadn't occurred to her that John would actually go on a date. She had often told him to go and find a new girlfriend but now she just felt strange. "Where did you meet her?"

"Through an online dating agency."

"You never told me. How long have you been talking to her?"

"For about a month and I didn't tell you because I thought you would laugh at me."

John sat on Steph's bed, laid down and put his head over the duvet. She pulled out her arms and put them around him and began to play with his hair. John had beautiful, thick hair but she had never before touched it and felt how soft it was. A few seconds later she heard him gently snoring gave him a shove, he toppled to the floor. "Sorry," she said "go to bed." But he was fast asleep so she crept to his room brought his pillow and duvet and managed to get the pillow under his head. As she dozed off she could hear his gentle snoring and felt a sense of peace and calmness. The next thing she knew was her alarm going off to start a new day.

Chapter Forty

They never spoke about that night. Steph went to work and the next few days she was busy getting to know what was now expected of her as a worker rather than a student. Alan came around each night but didn't stay over. He accepted that she needed some time getting used to the job.

John had some tempoary accommodation found for him in Manchester, a one-bedroomed flat. That Saturday in October was a strange time for Steph. She gave John a hug and kiss and waved him off.

As she shut the door Alan said, "Well now, at least for a while, we have the place to ourselves. I liked John but I suppose if I'm honest I was always a bit jealous of the times that you had alone with him."

"You didn't need to be," Steph said but as she said it she felt a blush go over her whole body.

Steph and Alan tumbled into bed but Steph didn't feel the way she had before.

"I arrived OK," John said, "it's a nice flat but guess what colour the bath is."

"Green," Steph chuckled.

"Of course, it just had to be."

John knew that Steph hated most green things. She said that green should be left outside for nature and not to be worn or sat on. John really wasn't bothered one way or the other but found her attitude generally rather amusing.

"I'll see you soon," Steph said.

"Yes, send me some good stories."

"OK, bye."

Steph knew that an episode in her life had come to an end. She would always know John but would never experience the closeness that she had enjoyed with him again. He had moved on and she was with the man she loved. With John away she realized that she did really love Alan. Alan was so sweet, he understood her so well and the next time she lay in his arms she knew that was where she wanted to be. When John found his woman she would be happy for him because she had found the love that she always wanted. Yes, she had loved Steve but, as Alan said, she knew now that he wasn't her intellectual equal. He just accepted the world as it was and couldn't see that there were things which needed challenging.

"I've got some work for you, Steph."

"Great, at last."

Steph had found the induction more interesting than she thought that she would but she was now glad that she could get down to some work.

"I need to have a little chat with you as well."

Steph felt uncomfortable when Martin said this; she felt as though she had done something wrong. She followed Martin into his office.

"It's Paul Landers," Martin said.

"Yes," said Steph knowing what Martin was about to say.

"You should have told us, Steph, that your fiancé was going to adopt him."

"He wasn't my fiancé at the time."

"Oh I see. Well, we must make sure that at work you have nothing to do with him or his family; you must make sure that he never rings you at work."

"OK," said Steph.

"I'll tell all the team and the secretarial staff so they know too."

Dennis didn't agree with what Martin had said and said so in front of Steph.

"That's discriminatory; that means Paul can't ring his mum at work. Every other kid can ring their mum or dad."

"It doesn't matter Dennis, just leave it."

"He can text her," said Marie.

"That's not the point."

The team had had members who had become partners but no one before in the team had adopted one of the clients. In fact, there was a rule that they couldn't. In Steph's case it was her partner who was adopting and now she was marrying him this was why she was adopting. Paul's social worker was in full favour after discussing the situation with Alan, Paul and her manager but she still had to go to the panel for their approval.

Steph got on with her work. To start with she had some fairly low-key cases which she worked with easily. Then one day, when she had been in post for about six weeks, Martin pulled her into his office and said, "Do you remember the Lewis family? You visited Jim and his family with Sarah."

"Yes," said Steph.

"Well, I need someone to work with Graham Lewis who is Mark Lewis's ten-year-old son. You would visit with Karen, our support worker. Did you work with Karen before? I can't remember."

"No, I saw her around but I never worked directly on a case with her."

"She's a very experienced worker and good at her job, you'll be fine with her."

"So you've got Mark Lewis have you?" said Dennis. "You know he's a complete loony; you met his brother Jim didn't you, well, he's tame compared to Mark but then you like a challenge, don't you?"

Steph wondered what she was going into, she picked up the phone and dialled the number.

"Hello, Mr Lewis, this is Stephanie Clover, I will be Graham's new social worker."

She arranged to meet with Graham and his family the next Monday afternoon.

Steph then rang the mother of one of her existing cases, a child with a severe disability, to see how things were going. She liked doing social work and although she feared what the team had said about Mark Lewis, she decided that she would keep an open mind; she wouldn't condemn him before she had even met him. This was just the way she was and she hoped that she would never change.

Chapter Forty-one

Pete moved in three weeks after John had left and brought some very strange ornaments with him from when he travelled as a young man in Africa. He said that he couldn't live without them but Steph found them rather spooky and so insisted on them being kept in his room. Pete was easier to get on with than she had expected. David continued to come around rather a lot and flirted with Pete.

"He's always here when Pete's here," Steph said to Alan one day, as he helped her fold up the sheets.

"Well invite Ian around a bit more then."

"No, I think that will make it worse."

Later that evening Steph chatted with Lucy on the phone and asked her what she thought.

"You've just got to leave them to it, you can't interfere. By the way, have you heard from John recently?" she said, quizzingly.

"Yes, he gets in touch every few days. I think he's OK. He's been doing some computer dating."

"And has he found anyone he likes yet?"

"No, I don't think so."

"Not surprising really, there's only one woman for him," she laughed. A shiver went down Steph's spine as she said this.

"Well, if you are implying that its me then he'll just have to go without. I have the man I love."

"I know, I was only joking. Your Alan is fab, you really won't get anyone better than him."

"I know," but Steph still had doubts and she thought about the night when she played with that soft, thick hair. She remembered that inner peace that she felt as she drifted off to sleep.

"Are you OK?" said Alan, as he came into the living room with a tray with drinks and some crumpets.

"I thought you might like some crumpets."

"Yes, yummy," Steph said, smiling at him.

"This is nice," said Alan, "just you and me."

"Yes, but it won't be like this very often with Paul around."

"It will when he is in bed though and we can..." Alan looked at Steph in a raunchy way.

"I've got the date for the panel," Alan said.

"I hope that it isn't difficult because of me being in the team. I might have to look for another job."

"We'll think about that after the panel; don't jump to conclusions, Steph. Martin has been very good making sure that you have nothing to do with Paul at work and once we have adopted him then the support comes from another team anyhow and his mum's social worker is based in another office."

"I know," she said as she cuddled up to him, "I suppose I'm just a little nervous about it, that's all."

"Come here," he said.

Steph felt safe in Alan's arms. He was right for her. He was so calm and level-headed. He had said that they were complementary and he was right; they truly were. And now she had no doubts. Her thoughts of John were just a silly fancy. She really loved Alan and knew that she would have a happy life with him.

"It will be strange suddenly being a mum to an eleven-year-old," Steph exclaimed.

"Yes, but we'll make great parents and Paul will be a great help when we have our little ones."

"Steph hadn't thought of children since she had split from Steve and now the prospect seemed a little daunting.

"Alan, I don't think I'm ready yet."

"There's no rush, we need to be parents to Paul first anyhow, and you are only thirty-one. There is still plenty of time."

The phone rang and it was Ian

"Is David round with you?" he said

"No," Steph replied.

"OK. If he turns up, will you tell him the kids are here?"

"Yes."

Steph replaced the handset.

"I reckon he's out with Pete, he got back from London late last night and disappeared off early this morning. By the way, Steph, we need to start thinking about where we are going to live."

"I know but not now, let's just chill out."

John liked being in Manchester but he missed Steph. He was determined to make a success of his new career as a scriptwriter. His freelance work was bringing him enough money to live off but he knew that until he produced an outline of the series that he would get little from the TV studio.

The head of series had agreed to meet him to discuss it further and so John was working hard on his bible of characters. He wanted to have as much control as he could. He didn't want it to be a watered-down second-rate series. John knew that social workers were working daily with some very interesting characters but he had to convince the boss.

He rang Steph every few days. He'd have liked to ring her more often but he knew that she had Alan and he just had to accept that they would never be more than friends. She had been instrumental in changing his life and making him see the world differently but now he had to go it alone. He would be a friend to Steph and Alan and uncle to Paul.

But when the wedding invite arrived the same day as he was going to see the big boss he had a mixture of feelings. He felt happy for Steph but also sad and lonely. He wanted to ring her and say, "Please marry me instead. Give me a second chance." But he stifled his thoughts and concentrated on the meeting with the big boss. He had to convince him that the public wanted a change. They had had enough of cops and docs and could now take on the no-win situations that social workers found themselves in.

Chapter Forty-two

Steph had been working with Graham Lewis for three months and she got on well with him. Mark Lewis wasn't as bad as everyone made out. She knew that he was pushing drugs but he never mentioned it when she was there and no strange visitors appeared. In fact, he said that he had a lot of respect for Steph.

"I know you are trying to do your best for our Graham and Steph, I really don't want him to turn out like me and Jim," he confided to her one day when she arrived at the house early when no one else was around.

"That's great Mark, I can't work miracles but I can at least try."

"There's something else I want to tell you but you mustn't breathe a word to anyone."

"You know I can't do that, I have to tell my boss so unless he can know you better keep it to yourself."

"I wonder what it was that he wanted to tell you Steph," Martin said as she discussed the situation in her supervision session.

"I don't know, he's obviously ready to spill the beans about something, I'll just wait for it to come out in his own time." "I'm really pleased with what you are doing with Graham and school are impressed too, well done. I'd like you to take on a new case, the Browns, which has just been handed over to us from the assessment team. Your friend Tom did the initial assessment and so you could talk to him about it. It concerns a mother with twin babies, a boy and a girl. There are suspicions that she is interfering with the baby girl or if she isn't someone in the family is. At the present she has just asked for some support but the health visitor isn't very happy with how the girl twin is developing. The health visitor is Janet Munroe, who you may know gets rather too worried too often about her babies as she calls them but Tom felt that this time she was probably justified in her concern. Could you liaise with Tom on the case and work it jointly initially?"

Steph left Martin's office feeling very pleased. Martin wasn't known to give praise lightly, a typical trait of social workers, and he had given her what looked like a really interesting case to add to her caseload.

"Good supervision then?" said Dennis

"Yes," said Steph, as she threw her diary in to her bag and rushed out of the office to her appointment, which she was already ten minutes late for.

"We need to talk about the wedding," Alan said.

"I thought that we had arranged everything," Steph replied.

"Most things but have you decided what you want me to wear or what you are going to wear yourself?"

"No, there's plenty of time for that."

"It's only six weeks away."

"I want you to give me a surprise, the same as I'll give you," Steph said.

"What time is John coming tonight?" Alan said.

"Teatime. He reckoned he was going to leave about three, he said."

"Will you be back from work?"

"He still has a key, he forgot to give it to me."

"That's OK then, I think I'll be a bit late tonight," Alan remarked. Alan lived half between his own house and Steph's house these days. He loved cuddling up next to her at night-time and missed her when he was at his own home. He had truly found his woman and when she or other people joked about him with other women he just wasn't interested. He never knew that he could love someone so much. For three years he had been bewitched by her, there was just something about her and now she wanted him he was so happy.

He was still a little uncomfortable about John and had small doubts but these had lessened since John had moved away. He wondered how he would feel seeing John and Steph together again. He admired Steph's ability to transform people's lives. Through his work as a lawyer he had come across a few people who knew Steph and they had sung her praises. He was so proud of her.

He had no doubts about being Paul's dad. Paul had asked him, if it was a choice between him and Steph who would Alan put first. Alan had honestly said that he would put Paul first. His friends thought that this attitude was strange but he knew that Steph was a survivor and that if he and Paul dropped down dead tomorrow then she would survive.

He went off to work happy, knowing that he had Steph to come home to.

Steph had a hectic day at work. She had to visit Jane Taylor, the mother of Giles, who was currently in hospital having yet another operation. His father had walked out a couple of months before leaving Jane to cope with Giles, who was severely disabled and at thir-teen was rather large to handle. She had a nine-year-old lad who was a lovely, helpful child and six-month-old baby twins. Steph had wondered how Jane had managed at the best of times but now that her husband had left she was more concerned. Giles was a difficult child who slept little at night. Jane's sister helped her out and would sometimes have the twins or their brother James overnight but she was working full time and had two children of her own. There was no other family to help out.

Steph was having a battle trying to get not only some more help for Jane from Social Services but also from the health service. Giles' condition meant that he had continuing nursing needs, as well as his difficult behaviour. Martin was in full support of what Steph wanted to do and felt for her frustration.

"I just don't know what else we can do," he said one day, when she was telling him for what seemed like the hundredth time about his needs.

Steph was also meeting with Graham. She wanted to try to get him to go to something like the Scouts so that he would mix with more children of his own age. Mark had felt that a lot of his problems were in the fact that he didn't have enough friends.

Steph also had her first visit to the Brown twins, Darren and Chloe. Steph thought how strange it was that she was working with two lots of twins. Tom said perhaps she would have twins too. Steph just laughed.

John zipped up his bag and thought about whether he had everything he needed for the weekend. He had had a good meeting with the boss and was feeling very excited. He had been given the go-ahead to write six episodes. They hadn't agreed a title for the series yet and he would pick Steph's brain about it.

He now felt fulfilled. He was writing about things that he could truly believe in. His book would have to go on a back burner but that didn't matter for a while, and he had been on a date.

The visit to the Brown's had been fine but Steph wasn't so happy about either her visit to Graham or Jane Taylor.

"I just couldn't do what she does," Steph said to Dennis, as she returned to the office.

"Steph, you can only do your best; we have so few resources, what else can we do?"

It was not only Steph and Dennis who felt helpless; it seemed as though the whole team felt that way. There was a general feeling of frustration and depression. Two of the team members had complaints against them. Martin was very supportive and reminded the team how many times they had survived before but the pressure was just becoming too great.

"We've got Steph's wedding to look forward to," Constance said.

A long discussion followed about what Steph should wear, as she really couldn't decide what it should be.

And then the phone call came.

Chapter Forty-three

Steph arrived home at 10.15pm. She had been at the hospital since 3pm.

Jane Taylor was in intensive care, one of the twins had been killed instantly the other was also in intensive care. Jane's sister, who had been driving the car, had been killed instantly.

Martin had come to the hospital with Steph and between them they had to try to sort out the three older children who were so distressed that Steph saw tears running down Martin's cheeks.

Steph was good in a crisis; it was afterwards that it hit her and as she drove home she found tears running down her cheeks. She had completely forgotten about John coming and had sent Alan a hurried text before she had to switch off her phone at the hospital.

She walked in the door and heard soft music coming from the living room. She remembered that John was there but couldn't face either John or Alan and so crept up to her bedroom and pulled her fleecy blanket over her. She drifted into a deep sleep she was so exhausted and then awoke wondering what day it was.

She went downstairs and found Alan in the kitchen. He came towards her and gave her a comforting hug.

"Oh, Alan," she bawled "it was so awful."

"Shh," he said, and cuddled her closer.

"John knows and will understand if you don't want to see him." Steph didn't reply. She released herself from Alan and walked towards the living room. John got up from the settee that they had spent so many nights giggling on and came towards her. She noticed that his hair had grown

She felt safe in his arms when he hugged her and didn't want to let go. It was John who let go and sat away from Steph. He knew that Alan was her man and that it was Alan that she needed now but his heart wished that he was the one who could comfort her.

Alan coaxed Steph to eat, but after two mouthfuls, although the cheese tasted nice, she couldn't swallow any more. She snuggled up to Alan and listened to their conversation.

"The TV series sounds great," said Alan.

"What TV series?" said Steph beginning to feel better. The clock struck twelve and Steph thought she had better go to bed.

"I'll tell you all about it tomorrow," John replied.

"Come on love, time for bed," said Alan.

Although Steph had fallen asleep for an hour she felt tired. Alan just cuddled her and didn't make any overtures towards her. She felt contented with just a cuddle.

The following day was hectic. Those tears at home had cleared Steph's head and she was now able to get on with the tasks in hand. The children had stayed with foster parents overnight. They had been fortunate to find foster parents who took all four, which was a very rare occurrence. Steph had been insistent that they should all be together but knew that this would only be the case as it was an emergency.

Jane was still seriously ill and Louise, her sister, had also been a lone parent. It was a complicated situation and Steph had to cancel all of her other appointments to sort it out.

Giles was supposed to be going home but the hospital had agreed to keep him in over the weekend. He had been rather fractious because he hadn't seen his mum but there was very little that Steph could do about that. The ward sister had moaned but Martin had reassured her that it would be given priority on Monday.

Steph also had a report to do for an emergency case conference on one of her other cases but she contacted the Chair of the conference who agreed to have it on Monday.

"It's just ridiculous," Dennis said, "if the public knew the stresses we were under perhaps they would be a little more understanding and less critical, but we just don't have the time or the energy to tell them."

Steph carried the three files to her car. She hoped that she had enough ink in her printer to print out the report when she had finished it. She had had four attempts to get the report done and each time she had a crisis to deal with and now, just the weekend when John had come to stay, she had a report to write.

The files she had inherited were so muddled that it was hard to follow the history. She felt disgruntled, but then she thought of Jane Taylor and how she had managed. She thought of Giles and how confused he must be. How could he possibly understand how his mum was and what would happen if she died? She began to panic, it was all too much, she couldn't cope. She took a deep breath, opened the car door and put the radio on. As she drove away the most strange thing happened; the oldie they played was "I Will Survive", and Steph sang along at the top of her voice and knew that she would survive, she would always survive. She had so much and she would regain her energy so that she could be there for Giles.

John wanted to tell Steph all about the TV series but she was too involved in the events of the last couple of days. He decided to write a piece for his journal about Steph and her dedication. He wrote about how, although she was detached, she felt for the family. Steph was a good social worker; she was there for the people she worked with, had a high degree of respect for them but was also honest. She wouldn't tell them that she could make everything right, she would guide them to a better quality of life.

John had half-heartedly done some computer dating but he didn't want to spend hours on the internet talking a loud of rubbish with some women, half of whom he believed were probably not serious anyhow.

He had been on three dates with different women. The first had brought along her married sister who was a lot more fanciable than she was. The second was about four stone heavier than she had described and so he thought should have been described as cuddly rather than average and the third seemed to be planning their wedding day on the first date. There was a nice girl that he had seen at the TV studio but he really didn't know much about her. Besides, he had one major problem – he just missed Steph and the more he wrote about her world of social work the more he missed her.

Alan just wanted to cuddle Steph all weekend but he knew that she had to get on with her report.

"Fancy a pint?" he said to John.

"OK."

"Steph, we're going down the pub so you can get on with your report."

"OK," a whisper came from the bedroom.

Steph always did her work on her laptop in her bedroom. She liked to be away from everyone. "Are you coming too?" said Alan to Pete. "Of course, I want to know how John, my old mate, is getting on."

Pete was still in London most of the time. He and David didn't seem to be seeing so much of each other.

Chapter Forty-four

Steph had just finished the draft of the report and popped to the kitchen to get a drink. The house seemed quiet without all of the boys, as she called them, at the pub. She would have liked to have gone, but knew that she had to get the report done. She felt pleased and was waiting for it to be printed out so that she could read through it.

She thought of the child that she had written about. David had been on the Child Protection register for emotional abuse for eight months and she new that at the conference they would be thinking of his future. He was four years old and Steph thought that he was a delightful child. He was an only child with a mother who was a career woman. David came second to her career. His dad was often away with his business, which took him abroad. There were grandparents but they lived over a hundred and fifty miles away and, although had been very supportive, didn't know how to help any more.

David had an amazing array of gadgets in his bedroom and he lived in an incredible house but when Steph went there she would think of the Lewis brothers and how they had been condemned for who they were.

When Mark Lewis had thumped Graham for being such a pain a case conference had been called and yet from birth David's parents had shown little interest in him and a textbook lack of bonding. It was when he changed nursery and seemed to be doing far less than the other children that concerns had been expressed, and that was when he was just two. It had taken some time for Social Services to get involved.

Steph thought of how hard it was to know what was the right thing to do. Before she trained to be a social worker she had raised money for Children in Need and had given money to the NSPCC. She had wanted the abuse to stop. But now she knew how hard it was to make it happen.

John, at breakfast that morning, had talked about the TV series and had described some of his key characters. She had fed back her comments about them, especially the one that sounded like herself who he wanted to put as the lead character.

"Oh, people might recognise that it's me," she fretted.

"But you said that you believed that you had to face the media and so that means that someone like you has to be the lead character. She doesn't have to look like you."

She had agreed that the character could be a bit like her but not too much.

Alan had laughed at the time and said that she was far too sensitive.

Now she finished the last sip of her drink and was just about to go back upstairs when the phone rang.

"Ian's left me," David wailed.

"Oh." That was all that Steph could say.

"Can I come round?"

"Of course you can."

"Is Pete there?"

"No, he's gone to the pub with Alan and John."

"Oh John's back is he? Steph, I don't want Pete to see me like this."

"Do you want me to come to you?"

"Could you?"

"I need to finish some work first. Oh, never mind, I'll do it later, I'll be round in a mo."

Steph wrote a note. "Boys, I'm at David's sorting out his latest trauma, see you later."

Alan sipped his Stella and thought, I like this. John really was a nice bloke. He had talked to them about his computer dating and the woman that he fancied at the TV studio and so Alan began to feel more relaxed.

The wedding was only a few weeks away and he and Steph had started talking about where they might like to live. Pete had showed an interest in buying Steph's house and the panel had been favourable to Steph being Paul's mum. He was happy, yes, very happy.

John thought Alan was a nice bloke. He could see why Steph was in love with him and felt pleased that she had made that decision. He could probably never give Steph what Alan could. He had wasted so much money when he lived in London and, although he had been more careful when he lived with Steph, he had found moving to Manchester much more expensive than he had originally thought. There was something else that he hadn't told anyone. He was feeling broody; yes, he'd like to have a kid, but there was no one to have one with. He wasn't looking for nubile twenty-two-year-olds any more; no, he would settle nicely for a woman in her thirties who had put a bit of weight on. He thought 11 stone-ish for a 5 foot 4 inch woman was fine but he didn't know whether he would cope with a 13 stoner. He knew he was being prejudiced but...

"Alan, could you fall for a huge woman?" he asked.

"Probably not," Alan replied honestly.

"But then again if I got to know someone over the internet and fell in love with them before I met them it might be a different story."

"But wouldn't she be lying to you... and wouldn't that be bad?"

"You hear such awful stories though," said Pete.

"Yes," Alan agreed.

"But there are success stories too," John countered.

"True, but I come across people in my work who have been duped and hurt."

"But surely that can happen in life anyhow," Pete commented.

"I suppose, but then you media men like to pick up the bad stories and scare us. I bet for every good story you tell there are

dozens of bad. You only have to listen to the local news; it's domi-
nated by bad stories," Alan said sarcastically

"Alan. You sound like Steph. She always used to go on like that.
Initially it irritated me, like people that go on about coincidences,
but after a while I began to see what she was saying. Steph could have
gone far in the media."

"She wouldn't want to, she leaves that to you," Alan smirked.

"I'm just popping to the bog," Pete said.

Now Alan was alone with John there were things he wanted to ask.
He had to know what John really felt for Steph, he just had to know.
"John, Steph has had an impact on both of us. She has made us see
the world differently. I like you John but I'm jealous of you and
Steph. I need to know what there is between you."

"We are good friends who had a brief fling, that's all," he lied.

"Are you sure?"

"Steph loves you Alan, she has always wanted you in her life. I was
just someone new and different. She wants to be with you and Paul."

John knew that this was the right thing to say and realized that, as
well as telling Alan, he was telling himself too.

Alan seemed relieved.

"Thanks," he said.

"For what?" said John.

"Just for that, but will you do something for me?"

"It depends what it is."

"If anything ever happens to me would you look after Steph, just
make sure she is OK and Paul too. I know that you will probably have
another woman in your life but will you encourage Steph to move on
and find happiness with another man?"

"Alan don't be so morbid, nothing is going to happen to you. You
and Steph are going to have kids and many years together. Yes, I
hope I find another woman but I've got to find the right one."

Pete returned to the table

"What are you two so intensely discussing, or can't I guess?"

Neither Alan nor John were listening, they were both in their
own worlds.

Alan was picturing his life with Steph whereas John was picturing his loneliness without her.

"Oh Steph, he said that I was flirting with Pete too much."

"Well you were," Steph replied.

"Oh it was harmless, you know how much I love Ian, I've told him so every day."

"Well, I really don't know what to say."

"What shall I do, Steph?"

"Go and see him."

"Will you come with me?"

"Where is he staying?"

"At his sister's, she rang to tell me that he was OK."

"Well, I can't go today, I have to finish my report and John is here. I've hardly seen him."

"What about tomorrow – please?"

"As long as we are not there too long. John is going back to Manchester on Monday morning."

"I'll ring Sally now and see if that is OK," David said.

David rang Ian's sister and agreed to go over for twelve o'clock the next day. It would be about an hour's drive to Sally's house.

"I'll drive," said Steph, "and then if you want to stay you can catch a train home."

Chapter Forty-five

The trip hadn't worked out the way that John had hoped.

The M6 was very slow on the drive back to Manchester. He had hardly seen Steph over the weekend. Sorting out David and Ian had taken much longer than she hoped as David had begged Ian to come back home and had been too tearful for Steph to leave. Eventually, Ian had agreed to come and Steph drove back with David talking non-stop.

It was hitting John hard, the realization that Steph was Alan's and would never be his. He hated thinking in this possessive way as he had learnt during his time with Steph that possessions meant little compared to people but he just wanted that sense of belonging. He had deluded himself. He had pretended that he didn't really want Steph but he did and his heart hurt. As he parked the car outside of his flat a sudden panic and air of loneliness came over him. He went into the flat. It felt warm and as he switched on the light he realized that he could cope. He had lots of work to do on the TV series and that's what he would do.

Steph went to work feeling tired. The weekend traumas had got to her. She knew that David and Ian had their upsets but this was the worst that she had had to deal with. She had rung David at eleven just before she went to bed to check if he was OK and he was. She had found Pete in the kitchen when she got up in the morning and had told him to keep away from David.

"Why should I?" he said.

"Because he couldn't handle you and because he loves Ian, that's why."

"Perhaps I fancy a fling. John told me you had had a fling together when you were going out with that Luke bloke."

Steph felt animosity towards Pete and wondered why she had agreed to him living there. John had been so easy to live with.

Alan had gone off early as he was in court and had a few things he needed to tie up first.

"I had better sleep at home tonight," he said, "this case is going to be pretty heavy."

"OK," said Steph, but after her brush with Pete she wasn't keen to be there on her own.

She arrived at work to find good news. A foster family had been identified for all four children to stay with. They were a couple with grown-up children and had a house with plenty of space. They were registered for two children but an emergency panel had been convened and they had been approved for the four children. Jane Taylor was still on the critical list and so somewhere had to be found for Giles.

Surprisingly, mid-morning, Steph got a call from Giles' dad to say that he would have him, for a while at least. Steph popped to the hospital to tell Giles the news.

"Where's Mum?" said Giles.

"She's very poorly at the moment."

"Is she going to die?" he asked.

"I don't think so but she might take some time to get better and so Dad wants you to live with him. What do you think, Giles?"

"Sounds great," he said.

"Phew, what a relief," said Martin. "By the way, the Dukes report..."

"What about it?"

"Well, some of the recommendations are not strong enough, we need to think about him being looked after."

"I never said that it wasn't an option. You haven't read it properly, I said that we needed to look with the parents at other options. Martin, the family have loads of money why can't they employ a nanny if they don't want to look after the kid themselves. You know what will happen if we go along the care line they will employ a clever lawyer and we will just look like fools. What have we got to offer the kid anyhow, there are so few placements?"

"Steph, you sound like me," Martin laughed.

"I'm just realistic that's all. We have these great idealistic views and I certainly support Michael's name staying on the register but what we can practically do for him? I don't know. Someone needs to give the parents a shake and say, 'He's your kid; you didn't need to have him. He needs love not things.'

"I'm sorry Martin but I find intelligent people who choose to have kids and then don't want anything to do with them just so... they make me want to scream sometimes. And then we have the narrow-minded bigots who stick all sorts of labels on the likes of Jim and Mark Lewis, the naughty boys, who never got over the fact that they came second to their mum's blokes..."

"It sounds like you need a holiday," Martin laughed.

"Or a doughnut," Sarah piped up.

"So who's buying then?" said Dennis. "Isn't it your turn Martin?"

"OK," said Martin.

Steph laughed and wondered how many social work teams lived on stodge or chocolate when they were stressed.

John decided to go on a new dating site. He wanted someone special in his life. Someone he could get to know gradually. He would look for someone who wasn't desperate and didn't rush into things and so he paid to be on the site for a year. He hoped that within a year he could find her.

As he was now an avid fan of Jane Austen he chose the name Captain Wentworth from the book *Persuasion*. He thought it was appropriate and liked the story of a love that was lost and found again. He wanted to find someone who had lost their greatest love and would find him. As he filled in the profile he found tears running down his cheeks. In two weeks time he would watch the woman he loved marry her good guy and he knew it would hurt but that he would be happy for her.

Steph went home and found a letter from John. He had sent some photos of the weekend and an outline of the pilot of his series.

He wanted her to give him a view of the characters and the outlined scenarios. He said that the company would pay her for her views.

Alan had suggested them going out for a meal but Steph had pigged out at the office and didn't really feel like much.

"I just thought it would do you good to get out a bit."

"Let's go swimming first," she said, "then I won't feel so guilty and might feel hungry."

"OK."

As she swam down the pool the last three years floated by. In two weeks time she would no longer be Stephanie Clover, although she had decided to keep the same name for work. She had thought of changing it but then thought that it would protect Paul and Alan from any nasties from her work. Paul had been officially adopted the previous week and they had a party to celebrate. Now they were getting ready for the wedding.

Lucy was to be her bridesmaid and looked stunning in the dress she had chosen. "If Tom doesn't get the hint in this he never will," she said.

Lucy and Tom had been together for some time now and were very happy but Steph knew that Lucy would really like to be married. She watched Alan swim up and down the pool and thought how much she loved him. Suddenly all of her doubts disappeared. How could she think that there was anyone else. He was just so right for her. He didn't make her laugh the same as Steve did and wasn't as good looking as John and didn't have such a great body, but to her he was gorgeous and loved her completely. He never seemed to look at other women.

One day he had walked in with some red roses and started singing "'Cos you're gorgeous…" The trouble was he got the tune wrong but that didn't matter. And in two weeks' time she would walk towards him and say "I will" and mean everything that she said.

Chapter Forty-six

Everyone introduced themselves at the Dukes case conference. The date had to be changed due to a crisis in the Dukes family. It had been a real nuisance as everyone had to be written to and phoned with the new information and trying to get an alternative date out of the Chair of the conference was so frustrating. Steph shared her frustration with Sarah, who she realized was better at bureaucracy than face to face work.

Steph asked Alan what he thought was more important, being able to talk with service users and find out what support they really needed or form-filling.

"Sadly, the form-filling seems to have taken priority recently," Alan said.

"We get the same, everyone does these days."

"But its just ridiculous and then, when we have to do all the form-filling, we get blamed for not visiting people enough. Some team members who have been in social work for twenty years remember the days when children on the Child Protection register had to be visited every week now they have to be visited every six weeks. I know that we have core groups every month but sometimes parents don't attend or we have to arrange transport for them to get to the office. It's just bureaucracy gone mad."

Steph found herself moaning a lot about things recently and today she wasn't in a good mood. She felt that the Dukes were not really working with her. Like all parents, they hated their child being on the register and at times she wondered what the point was too but at least she got a right to visit him and follow his development.

He had been tested to see if he had any form of disability and he hadn't, he was just neglected emotionally. He was not a very good mixer at school, which he had recently started and had no one to play with at home. Steph had mentioned the nanny idea to the Dukes but they said that it would cost too much money. They had a four-week holiday booked to the West Indies which they said that they both desperately needed and one of the grannies was coming to stay at the house to look after David as they thought that they needed a break from him. Steph found it so hard to understand this level of selfishness. He hardly saw them as it was.

The conference went OK but nothing changed, no more support – just the same until the next conference, which would be six months away.

"How did it go?" said Alan, as he rang to see if Steph wanted to go to the theatre that night.

"Sometimes I wonder what I am actually achieving."

That afternoon she met with Graham Lewis at school and then took him home. On the way home they chatted in the car.

"Did you know that Dad is going to college?" he said.

"No," Steph replied, rather surprised. "What is he doing?"

"He's learning to be a chef; you know that he's always liked cooking."

They arrived at the house and as they walked in Steph noticed that the windows were open and that stagnant smell had disappeared. Mark was in the kitchen doing some ironing.

"I hear you are at college now," Steph said as Mark made them a drink.

"Yes, I started three weeks ago and I love it."

"So the kids are going to get some good meals then."

"We always did," said Graham. "Dad is a great cook."

Steph went back to the office feeling really happy. She was so pleased with the relationship between Graham and his dad. In fact, the whole family seemed so much happier; she really felt that her straight, honest approach had made the family realize that they could change, and the consequences if they didn't. She wanted to recommend the children coming off the register but wouldn't yet as then they might not get any support and she didn't feel that they were quite strong enough to go it alone.

There seemed to be a pattern in social work where people asked for help and, by the time real help rather than piecemeal help was given, what was a difficulty had become a crisis. She understood why; it was the increasing amount of bureaucracy and however much individuals tried to tell the government how unnecessary a lot of the paperwork was it seemed not to get through to them. But for now she was pleased and it made up for the case conference.

Steph was trying to get up to date with her work so that she could have a good wedding and honeymoon not thinking about work.

She didn't go home every night worrying about people but some nights she would wake up from a deep sleep and have to climb over Alan to get out of bed to write herself a message because of some important thing that she had forgotten to do. He would mumble something and then go back to sleep. Last night she had woken up, realizing that she had forgotten to ring the hospital to seen how Jane Taylor was.

"Oh damn," she said.

"What?" said Alan

"Oh, I forgot to ring the hospital and that ward sister is difficult at the best of times."

"Never mind," said Alan. "Go back to sleep love, you'll sort it."

Alan turned over and gave Steph a cuddle; she relaxed in his arms and felt a warm glow. She felt that she was the luckiest woman in the world. She had an interesting, if challenging job, a nice house and best of all a man who she really loved and who loved her.

Chapter Forty-seven

"Steph, I want to call you Mum but Mum's not happy about it, she says its OK to call Alan Dad but doesn't want me to call you Mum."

"That's OK, Paul, I never expected you to call me Mum. How is Mum anyhow?"

"She's doing well, she's been off the drugs for several months and Charlene and Dwayne have visited her four times."

"Great and are you happy with Dad taking you over there every other weekend for the day?"

"Yes, I like going but after a few hours I want to come home as I'm bored. I can't wait until we get the new house."

"Yes, it's a pity we couldn't move in until after the wedding but you are happy living here til then, aren't you Paul?"

"I'd rather live at Dad's house where I've got my things."

"OK, I'll talk to Dad about it."

Alan had thought that it would be better to live at Steph's house as there were more kids for Paul to play with locally but he agreed with Steph that it really wasn't worth unsettling Paul.

John had shut himself away for a month and woke up that morning realizing that he had nothing to wear to the wedding, which was only a few days away. He had been busy writing, the characters had flowed and the boss seemed keen on his storylines. They wanted to go into production in the spring and so that still gave him time. He had been told that if the pilot was successful that there would be other

173

scriptwriters to help develop the characters and he would be in charge of the storylines, but he still hadn't got a title.

As well as Steph, he was using stories in the press to develop his characters. He now saw what Steph had been trying to tell him about – the hard, cold reporting that for so long he had been a part of.

From time to time he would have a break and search the dating sites to see if there was anyone that he fancied. Occasionally he would email someone and he had spoken to a couple of women on the phone but had not met up with anyone else. The woman at the studio that he fancied turned out to be in a long-term, happy relationship.

Some days he would think of when he lived with Steph but he knew that there was really no point going along with those thoughts. She had made her choice and he believed that Alan was the better man for her but as the wedding drew near he began to panic that the calls that he so relished from Steph when she would talk excitedly about what she was doing would become fewer and further between.

It had been a pig of a day. Everything that Steph had planned had been upset and she had spent most of the day trying to find somewhere for a sixteen-year-old girl, who had been looked after since she was thirteen, and her eighteen-year-old boyfriend to live.

"Are you Social Services?" one guest house had said.

"Yes," Steph replied. "We don't have any druggies here," the voice said and promptly put the phone down on Steph.

"Aargh," Steph exclaimed.

"No luck then," said Martin, who had been as helpful as he could.

"This is just ridiculous," exclaimed Steph.

Eventually they managed to find a B&B that would take them for two nights but Steph knew that then the search would start all over again. She felt guilty that someone else would have the burdensome task as she would be on her honeymoon. She was having Friday off and was getting married the next day.

As she drove home that night the last few years seemed to flash by her. Tonight she was going on her hen night. Lucy was arranging everything and it was to be a surprise. John would stay with her at the house while Paul and Alan would stay at Alan's.

"Its traditional," said Steph's mum and so they had agreed to it.

Steph hadn't seen John for ages and so was looking forward to seeing him. He had said that he would arrive at 5.30pm and so she had agreed to meet him at the station.

"My train is going to be half an hour late," John's text said. "Will you still pick me up or not?"

"Yes," Steph texted back.

She decided to stay at the office and catch up on some of her write-ups. She wouldn't have long to get ready but then she knew that they were going for a meal and so had told John that he would have to sort himself out a meal.

The train pulled into New Street Station. It had sat in the tunnel for what seemed to John like ages, as he stood in the queue waiting to get off. The woman in front of him had a large bag, two small children and a pushchair and so he had offered to get the bag off for her which she had readily agreed to. He wondered how she managed. The oldest child was only about three and the other child was not yet walking.

John's broodiness came to a sudden halt as he descended the steps and took out his small and the large bag. He saw Steph coming towards him and an electric shock passed through his body. How could he ever love anyone else, he thought.

Chapter Forty-eight

"Oh no," said Steph giggling as the stripogram came towards her. She couldn't really work out who he was supposed to be.

"Oh, Lucy," she giggled.

"Hi John," she slurred as the taxi dropped her off back at home.

"So, it was a good night then?" said Pete. "I'm off to bed," he murmured as he went up the stairs.

"Tell me all about it then," said John.

"What did you do?" Steph asked.

"I went to the pub with Pete and his new fellah, have you met him yet?"

"No."

"Guess what he does?"

"Policeman?" said Steph.

"Yes, how did you know?"

"I just guessed, that's all, I reckoned that Pete had a yearning for a uniform." She giggled as she collapsed on the settee.

"Come here and give me a cuddle," she said.

"No, you're too pissed," John said.

"Frightened I might jump you," she giggled.

"I might take advantage of you," he said.

"Nah," Steph slurred.

"Come on Miss, it's bedtime," John said and helped Steph up the stairs. She seemed a dead weight. He got her into her bedroom and she fell with him onto the bed.

"Give me a kiss," she said and John found himself being kissed by Steph and enjoying it.

"We had a good time, you and me, in London didn't we?" said Steph, as John left the room.

"We did," he said and he shut the door and went back downstairs to sleep on the settee.

"Oh my head" said Steph, "I bet I was awful last night."

"You were quite funny actually," said John. He decided not to remind Steph of the kiss. It would only upset her and that was the last thing that he wanted to do. He loved her too much for that.

Friday was a whiz of last-minute preparations. Paul was a bit of a nuisance because his mum phoned up in a drugged state and said that she was going to a solicitor so that he could come back and live with her.

"Steph, I don't want to go," he cried down the phone.

"You won't be," she said.

"We are your parents and your mum is your mum."

"Mum says that you won't let me see her."

"You know that's not true."

"Can I go and see her today? Please?"

"OK, put Dad on the phone."

Steph was irritated but she knew that unless she let Paul go that he would be a nuisance for the rest of the day and both she and Alan would be tired before the wedding started.

"OK, Steph, I'll ring her now," Alan said.

John had been nearby and overheard the conversation. He was making toast at the time and as he put marmite on it he thought what a giving person Steph was. It was the day before her wedding and instead of getting herself ready she was sorting out her adoptive son's natural mother. He wondered how many other people would do this. He would certainly write this into one of his storylines.

Steph had given him a rundown of some of her cases. She was always careful not to give information that would identify who the real people were and often she talked not so much about the cases themselves as what was expected of her and her colleagues. Most people when their day was finished could go home but social workers were regularly in different dilemmas about their clients and would feel guilty spending the same money on a Chinese take away as many had to feed a whole family.

John looked at Steph and, for an instant, wanted to tell her how he felt, but then surely she knew and she had made her choice. No, he had to accept that he had blown it. He had been so cocky, he could get any woman but when he realized that Steph was the woman he really wanted it was too late.

The day he married Wendy he had looked at Steph standing next to Luke and had been jealous. Now he just felt a strange mixture of happiness and sadness. He was happy for both Steph and Alan but so sad for himself. Yes Steph would always be his friend, he knew that but if only he hadn't been such a fool and maybe she would have been more.

Chapter Forty-nine

Alan and Paul went to see Paul's mum. Alan said that he would be back in an hour as by now it was 8pm and the drive back home took three-quarters of an hour.

He decided to go to Asda and buy a few things that they needed at home. As he walked around the shop he remembered the day he had met Steph and how quiet she had been in the coffee bar. In fact, all his memories came flooding past. He remembered what a fool he had been when he had listened into her conversation and she had angrily told him about her ex's baby. He had fancied her so much and her wild outburst instead of putting him off had just enhanced those feelings. He had been so correct about the tutor/student relationship that when he found himself falling in love with her and longing for the next time that he could bump into her he knew that he had to get away.

But it just hadn't worked, perhaps he should have tried for longer. There were women in the States who blatantly showed their interest in him but then if he'd stayed he wouldn't be sitting here today.

He had been jealous of John. He knew that Steph had had a fling with him. She had told him that it was all linked to her feelings about Steve. She had found it so hard to get over him, but he was now certain that it was him that she loved and it sent a warm feeling through his body.

He was looking forward to their times together. Friends had asked why he had continued to adopt Paul when it was likely that he and

Steph would have kids but he was loyal and there was just something about Paul. His mum said, "He's your kid, he even looks like you and is beginning to have your mannerisms."

He sipped his coffee and looked at his watch, he had ten more minutes before he would have to leave to collect Paul.

"I'll miss this," said Steph, as she and John sat close together on the settee.

"You'll have Alan to sit next to instead."

"Yes," she said.

"Are you having regrets, Steph? You are doing the right thing, you know."

Steph hesitated in her reply. "I think its just memories of what happened with Steve that's all. Just think, I might have married you," she laughed.

John felt a flush go over his face as she said this and said in his head "If only" but aloud "What a fool you would have been."

"Maybe," Steph replied. This unsettled John. Was Steph not sure? He wondered whether he should tell her how he felt.

The phone rang.

"You're back, thank goodness," Steph said, as Alan told her of the visit to Paul's mum.

"That's it," thought John. "My last chance gone forever." He crept out of the room leaving Steph talking on the phone and went into the kitchen, he opened up his laptop and wrote.

"Love you too," Steph said as she put the phone down. John had gone whilst she was talking to Alan. She went in the kitchen and found him busily tapping away on his laptop.

"Is everything OK?" he said, looking up.

"Yes, apparently Paul's mum was really nice and had a present waiting for me and Alan."

"Rather a strange way to give you a present."

"I think she felt a little left out but it just would have confused Paul inviting her to the wedding."

"Oh, Steph, you weren't going to were you?"

"I had thought about it. Oh, and Alan had too, but we had been advised against."

"You mad fools," he laughed.

"So what are you writing about now?"

"Oh nothing in particular and I still haven't got a name for the programme, it's so difficult and frustrating."

"Well, I'm off to bed," Steph said, coming over and giving John a kiss on the cheek.

"Night, my love," John said, kissing her back and continuing to write.

Steph undressed and thought of what John had said, so naturally, so absent-mindedly. Did he really love her and was she still in love with two people? The man that she had wanted for so long and the man she had lived with and had been so happy to come home to; surely not.

Chapter Fifty

It was a bright sunny morning. Steph looked at the clock, which said 6.15am. She had been waking herself up throughout the night and now decided that she wouldn't try to go back to sleep again. They were getting married at twelve o'clock and, although neither of them were church-goers, for some reason they had decided on this tradition and had visited St Peter's Church as instructed.

Lucy had helped Steph choose her dress. She had gone for the traditional white but wasn't going to wear a veil. Instead, she was having coloured braids in her hair. The hairdresser had assured her that they would look lovely but now Steph wasn't sure. Her appointment was at 9.30 so she had plenty of time.

Steph opened the curtains and decided just to lie for just a while. This would be the last time as, after the honeymoon, they were to live in Alan's house until the move to the new house.

There was a knock on the door and John walked in with a tray full of goodies. "Morning, miss," he said. "This will be the last time I will be able to say this," he laughed.

"Oh, lovely John."

"Champers, madam?" he said as he opened a bottle and poured some into a glass.

"Aren't you having some too?" Steph exclaimed.

"No, this is all for you. Which would modom like first strawberries or chocolate croissants?"

"Strawberries, I think," said Steph giggling.

"Shall I pop one in modom's gob?" John said, in a distinctly false accent.

"Go on then," Steph giggled.

As she lay in her bath Steph knew that this was going to be a wonderful day and she had no doubts at all. Alan was the man that she wanted to spend the rest of her life with but she would always want to know John too.

Time went rushing by and Steph chatted to Lucy as she had the braids put in her hair. The hairdresser was right, they did look nice. John put on his suit and appeared by the front door.

"Blimey, Steph, are you marrying the right guy?" she said, laughing.

"Of course she is," said John.

The house was now full of people, Steph's parents and sisters, aunts, uncles and then they were all off, leaving Steph and her dad waiting for the car.

"You look gorgeous," her dad said, "and Alan is a great guy. I did wonder whether it would have been John, as you are so close, but I think you've picked a fine man in Alan and he obviously loves you to pieces."

"Yes, and I love him too Dad," Steph replied.

The bells rang and Steph felt that she was floating on air. Her nerves had settled as she walked up the aisle with the soft music playing.

John looked at her as she passed and thought how, if it had been him marrying, her they would have played "'Cos you're gorgeous..." just because she was. But he smiled at her as she passed and gave an outward appearance of happiness. He was happy but sad too.

Steph threw the bouquet straight at John and he caught it. Everyone cheered but a strange cold chill went down John's spine. Was it memories of his own wedding or something else? But he knew that he couldn't keep the flowers.

"You have them," he said to Lucy, as the car drove away. "There's no one that I want to marry."

Chapter Fifty-one

It was hard getting up to go to work that wet Monday morning. Steph had had a fantastic time and now she was back in the real world. Paul couldn't find his PE kit and Alan had a cold.

"So this is what family life is about," Steph said to Helen, the receptionist, as she collected the pile of post out of her slot.

"Welcome back," said Helen, with a grin on her face. "So are you now Stephanie Taylor or are you keeping Clover for work?"

"I've decided to keep Clover, partly because of what Alan does, he might be a judge one day, you know."

"And then you'll be able to give up work and be a lady of leisure."

"Me, give up social work? What would I do with myself?" Steph laughed.

Steph soon got back into the swing of things and was so pleased to see that Graham and his dad were still doing so well. She had a busy caseload but going home to Alan's cuddles and encouragement more than compensated for the work pressures. She was so happy that sometimes she felt that she would burst. Paul began to do well at school.

Lucy and Tom had decided to get married. They said that after seeing Steph and Alan it gave them the push to make the plunge. Everything just seemed great and Steph could fully enjoy life and this seemed to rub off on her service users, who were turning their lives around too.

"You getting married has injected hope into the team," Martin said one day.

187

"How long is it now?" he said.

"Seven months," said Steph.

"So is it babies next?" said Phil.

"Stop being so sexist," said Sarah.

"I was only asking."

"Maybe," said Steph. "Who knows?" she giggled.

John had decided to make a real effort on the dating sites and had been on a date with a woman who he had known for a while. It hadn't been too bad and he decided to meet with her again. Besides, he hadn't had any sex for ages and wondered whether he'd remember how to do it again. Steph had been so busy since she had been back settling back into work and Paul had been in trouble with a couple of kids at school and so John decided not to ring so often. Nowadays Alan would often answer the phone and it just didn't feel the same. The months went by and he realized that his relationship with Steph had changed forever.

He got himself ready for the date and decided that he would put on some body spray that Steph had given him last Christmas. He drove to the restaurant that they had agreed to meet at and sat waiting for Suzie to arrive. She walked towards him looking very attractive. They chatted and the evening went well until they chose their puddings.

"What would you like?" said John.

"Strawberries, I think," she said.

The strawberries arrived and suddenly John felt a chill.

"Are you OK?" she said.

"Yes" he said, but just felt that there was something wrong.

"Are you sure?"

They finished the meal and went their own separate ways. John arrived home to find the police on his doorstep.

Chapter Fifty-two

"The Birmingham Police have been in touch with us; your friend Stephanie Taylor needs you, I'm afraid there has been a tragedy."

"What's happened?" said John panicking.

"Her husband and son have both been murdered."

"What?"

John couldn't take in what the police were saying. Apparantly Alan had taken Paul to visit his mum and when he came to collect him a few hours later there were some drug dealers in the house and in the affray Alan had tried to protect Paul but both he and Paul had been shot.

"I'll come straight away," he said.

John threw some clothes into a bag and shut the door behind him. The journey from Manchester to Birmingham seemed to take forever. He arrived at Alan's house and knocked at the door. Steph's dad opened the door and welcomed John through his tear-stained face. Steph's mum was cuddling Steph as she cried in a mournful way. The tears ran down John's face.

"What can I do?" whispered John to Steph's dad.

"Just be here for her," he said. "That's all that any of us can do."

But there was more. As the press arrived on the doorstep, John was there to tell the truth. He told them how this beautiful woman, who was so dedicated to her career, had fallen deeply in love with a man who lived that dedication too by trying to give an eleven-year-old boy a second chance in life but that they had been beaten.

He now knew that he had to tell the truth even if the truth hurt. No longer was it good enough to blame others; and he would always be there for Steph.